THE
BACHELOR MACHINE

THE
BACHELOR MACHINE

M. CHRISTIAN
with an introduction by Cecilia Tan

GREEN CANDY PRESS

The Bachelor Machine by M. Christian
ISBN 1-931160-16-3
Published by Green Candy Press
www.greencandypress.com

Copyright © 2003 by M. Christian
Cover photograph © 2003 by Larry Utley
Cover model: www.piercedangel.com
Cover and interior design: Ian Phillips

Printed in Canada by Transcontinental Printing Inc.
Massively Distributed by P.G.W.

For Jill,
and our wonderful future.

CONTENTS

INTRODUCTION

I'm going to tell you a secret. There are only two people in the world I envy. One is the late Roger Zelazny, whose talent for an almost jazz improvisational way of writing I could never match. The other is M. Christian, for writing exactly what I'd write if only I could get off my ass. Which is to say, raunchy hallucinatory sexfuture dreams that never fail to arouse me and kick me in the gut at the same time. Good stuff.

I've always said if there was someone out there who would write exactly what it was I wanted to read, I wouldn't have to do it myself. Honestly, when I discovered M. Christian, I had that half-formed thought: gee, maybe I can quit... (of course, I didn't).

It was the summer of 1994, if I remember correctly. I had founded Circlet Press three years before, to fill a void in the literary world. At the time, there was nowhere to publish erotic science fiction, or futuristic erotica, or whatever label you want to put on the wild, genre-bending stuff I and Lauren P. Burka and others were writing. So I became a publisher, starting with chapbooks and slim little volumes of under 100 pages. As news of the press spread to other speculative sex writers, manuscripts had begun to pour in for our anthologies. I decided I needed help getting through the growing slush pile and cajoled Lauren and some of my other authors to sit in my one bedroom apartment one afternoon and read, read, read. We ordered Chinese take-out and delved into the manuscripts, pausing from time to time to eat a crab rangoon or read a "clunker" aloud. There were a lot of clunkers that day, and we were a pretty raucous group.

Then everything got quiet. I looked up from the story I was reading, and two of my readers were looking at each other. They then traded manuscripts: "Here, now you read this one, I want that one!" They'd found not one, but two, really good somethings. Lauren then brought the manuscript in her hand to me and strongly suggested I read it that instant, not later. "Just read the first sentence."

I saw the words: "I almost lost my virginity at fifteen, but his batteries ran low" and was hooked.

The manuscript was "Technophile" by M. Christian. Lauren had written on the comment form she handed me with it: YES YES YES. I agreed. It wasn't just the best story we'd read all day, it was one of the best stories we'd read in the genre, ever.

The other story we received that day was "State," a story I liked so much, I've published it twice. These two began a slew of stories Circlet published from Chris. At slush-readings in the future, people would go HUNTING for his name on envelopes, hoping to be the first to read something new. I'd like to say I had to break up a fistfight when "Fully Accessorized Baby" was discovered, but that would be the fiction writer in me trying to sensationalize. (We just took turns.)

When the story "Heartbreaker" came in, my then assistant Susan Groppi read it without knowing who it was from. "A very very very good story," she wrote in her comment form. "I often find I can't describe what it is I like, just that it's good." Her editorial instincts were right on—when a story just kicks ass, your initial reaction isn't a critical one, it's simply "woo hoo!"

One of the reasons I bought so many stories from Chris over the years is not only that the stories are consistently great, but that he has been able to write for any sexuality, from any point of view, man, woman, alien, third gender, robot, robot-wannabe... and of course sexualities and identities yet to be invented. For me, the whole purpose of combining two often formula-bound genres, erotica and science fiction, was to break out of the expected molds, to create something exciting, arousing, and provocative in all senses of the word. Chris has done that better than most who have tried their hand at it. He has a gift. And through that ability to see the world as it is not, to envision things wholly beyond our real boundaries of gender, technology, and identity, he is able to create characters that grab me. Characters I believe in. I empathize with Kusa, the rebuilt cybernetic woman-cop in "Heartbreaker." I want to fuck Fields "the perfect love doll" in "State" and see if I can crack her facade.

Even better, Chris is one of the few writers who has been able to sell me stories where everything is not happy and rosy. I've always insisted on a sex-positive outlook for Circlet Press—no rape, no dismemberment, no homophobia, you get the idea—but the result is a lot of happy stories, where sexy people have good sex and both they and the reader enjoy it. The problem here, from a literary standpoint, is that without conflict, there's not much of a story. Chris is one of the best at creating the kind of conflict that works best in an erotic story: inner conflict. The kind of conflict that many a writer has shied away from because it is the most difficult kind to portray believably and intriguingly. The kind of conflict that in science fiction is all too often replaced by external action, a fight, a battle, an explosion. This is why an M. Christian story is not just some of the most excellent, cutting-edge erotica around, but also great science fiction.

This is also why Chris' stories quickly found homes outside of the specialized niche of Circlet Press. I started seeing his name in anthologies like Best American Erotica and The Mammoth Book of New Erotica. Since then, I find it hard to name an erotica market or anthology that he is NOT in. The secret is out—I don't think Chris' manuscripts even go to any-one's slush pile anymore. (These days they don't even go to my office; I take them directly into the bedroom.)

There's one more person I envy, and that's the reader who is picking up this book for the first time. Prepare your-self to discover the intense pleasure within.

Cecilia Tan
Cambridge, MA

Cecilia Tan is the author of The Velderet, Black Feathers, *and* Telepaths Don't Need Safewords. *Her stories have appeared in* Ms., Penthouse, Best American Erotica, Best Lesbian Erotica, *and many other places.*

STATE

Once part of a sprawl of temporary industrial units floated into Kyushu harbor to make a Korean-owned nanochip factory, the building was industrial architecture that had been stuck on a shelf and left to rust. As far as Fields knew—and could see—rust still managed the property. Rumors said that Mama had scored the old building for cheap, had found some hungry jacks to scalp juice from the main grid and some mysterious "sources" for the rest. The girls? They came from wherever lost girls always came from: the cramps of hunger or addiction, the Devil of father. They came and Mama fed them, sprayed them when they were sick, and put that rusting roof over their heads. In return, they worked.

Friday nights weren't usually this busy. There were even rumbles from Mama's office that Fields might be called down from her box to work the cribs with the pie-faced girls. But someone asked for the special of the house and she was spared having to watch the ordinary flatscreen with the rest of the girls. She *was* the special, so she had a while to get ready and even watch the end of *Don't Drop It* (her favorite) on the antique Hakati tank and—*yum!*—relish the new host).

The antique took a long time to power down, and she always (since Mama had sold it to her) felt that thrill-tingle of worry that some client would come in and still see the spray/wash/float of green/blue/red hanging in front of her cheap holo print of *Tokyo At Night* that masked the unit and ponder a bit too long over why a Mitsui Automaton would be watching a game show.

The streets, and common knowledge, said that Autos took a while to power up, boot up their software, get their circuits warm and ready, though never really *willing*: the perfect love doll. The perfect toy. The *real* fact was that it took Fields time to get completely into her Act.

Her friendly gray robe went first, into the hidden closet behind the false wall of phony blinking telltales and dummy flatsceens playing loops of technical gibberish, with the rest of her reality; hung on a hook next to her vid discs, street clothes, wigs, pills, towels, creams, sprays, and plain-faced bottles of special dye.

Very special; an incredibly durable bonding polymer that she applied each morning, always careful to examine every inch of herself in a roll-up plastic mirror, lathering on the thick blueness at the faintest signs of her real pinkness before the light over the door flashed green. Her hair, every brown strand, was months gone—and kept at an imperceptible level by a chilling spray of tailored enzymes. Sure, she could wear any of her wigs, and sometimes did for those who just couldn't deal with a too-inhuman Automaton, but for the most part she liked going smooth and streamlined: they paid for a machine.

The little yellow hexagon pills still had about another two hours to go—her skin texture and temperature would be just *that* different. Not quite human, almost machine synthetic. Anyone, of course, who knew the real Mitsui would know the reality of pink-skin-and-blood Fields under the blue, behind the contacts, beyond the reengineered body. But then the Autos were very rare, their legends and rumors huge, and who would know the real thing, after all, in the dim shadows of big, sprawling, bad Kyushu?

Fields's body was a gift from Mama, really an investment. Those long days two years ago with the Osaka Scalpers had taken what nature had lucked her with and shaped her into an almost perfect Auto Class B—still one of Mitsui's most popular models. Strong shoulders; round face with high, almost too-wide-for-nature cheekbones; tiny, pert, full lips; huge crystal blue eyes; high, wide and moderate tits, huge against her actually small frame, with aggressively large nipples—some of it was really hers, some was machine made for her machine act. Her looks, real or made, would be good and profitable as long as the real unit was State-of-the-Art...and the rumors of how good, and how hot, kept flying.

Fields's cortical jack was a gift from Sammi, now long gone—his gift of matched wet dreams through cheap Kobe scalp implants was also gone. One quick brain-trip with the tall and lean New Tokyo hustler had been enough for the preteen Fields (spasms of her riding him, his impression of nothing-but-sex nothing-but-sex and her always on *fucking* top) running/stomping all over her images of that one time, that one *good* time at that Osaka shrimp stick stand when he had just smiled at her. The jack was the one and only thing that really remained of him. It was important to the Act, so she kept it polished and in good repair. The clients knew, if they knew anything, that no one had shrunk the hardware for the Autos enough for them to be self-supporting. They expected and got her—Regulation Blue, hairless, eyes also blue but no irises; just slightly cool, perfect little ass; perfection tits; and her braid of trailing cables. She was a love-doll lifted from Japanese collective consciousness, a manga sex toy—all eyes and ass and tits and mouth and cunt. Pure fantasy, rolled off the assembly line to a male libido's factory specs. Her body was flesh, tricked by drugs and chemicals—the jack on the crown of her head was real, the line was dead, but she was still State: the perfect whore, the perfect trick, perfect in her Act.

And, god knew, she liked it. Liked it a lot.

The fountain of basic colors died, and with it Fields's ritualistic fear of discovery. She sat on the stool, made sure one last time that she was jacked into the dead line, and that her breathing was cool and calculated. Mama buzzed to notify her that the client was coming up the stairs.

Green light over the door.

He was nice. She had been there, in that maze of old modular sheeting and drop-in offices, long enough to know it. That night, that Friday, she was tingling with work lust, and she liked it. *Don't Drop It* had that great new host, the one that rang of Sammi, her Tokyo hustler, when he was cruising and straight, and she had enjoyed a quick little jill while watching—running a blue finger up and down her little blue slit, bathing her blue pearl with her own juice. No cry, no come, not enough time for that. But a trembling thrill up and down her, up from her blue pussy, vibrating her back and jigging her leg. She was wet for the client, always wet for him (Mama's schooling), but she was going to be *really* wet for this one.

And he was going to be a good one. Mama's school and her years there clicked through her as he opened the door and came in. Shy and kind of reserved. He looked everywhere but where she sat on her stool in all her blueness, the Act full-blown: a square room, walled with semitransparent white plastic, bare save for the stool, a simple futon, one wall the brains of the Mitsui Automaton, and the "Unit" itself sitting on that black and chrome stool waiting for the Job—almost lifeless, almost perfectly human (Regulation Blue, so if they should impossibly break free they could never pass), waiting to do just what you wanted. Anything. At all. Your heart's desire, your cock's (and sometimes clit's) desire.

She stood up and took a neutral position, making sure her legs were just-so parted enough so he could see her blue slit and the dot of her blue clit. Her nipples were hard from her near-jill and Mama's school, and she knew her scent was filling his nostrils. Perfectly lifelike. Perfect imitation of a machine that was supposed to be better-than-lifelike.

He was a surprise. Still a type, but still a surprise. Away from the Company tour, maybe? Shy and inside about this, maybe not wanting to be seen with the rest of his Contacts diving into perfumed pools and being given tepid blow jobs by bored/hungry girls? What better way to do the same kind of acts without the examining eyes: find someone who didn't care, who couldn't shoot him down by batting her dull, professional eyes.

"Stand up and come here." Stone-cold, gravelly, deep. Young, yeah, but childish, no way.

As Fields stood and walked in that special loose-hipped caricature that the Autos really did walk, she took better stock of Johnny. He was maybe mid-thirties. His synthetic suit was simple and professional. The tie, though, was real silk and the scenario changed. And the tone, the strength, the gravel: maybe he was one of the managers, out to do something special with someone who couldn't complain or say no...to anything.

Didn't believe it was possible, but Fields got even wetter. She liked it rough and fast and maybe metal-tinged dangerous. And she was in the mood, anyway. She liked her job, the other girls for the most part, and the customers quite a bit.

"How can I please you, sir?" It had taken her a while to get the voice just right: just enough of a noninflection. Mama's School. The Medicos. And something that was just part of the Act.

The programs were varied, and rumors circulated. The Units, the Autos were soft and hardwired to be the best—they could surprise you, so Fields was loose in her Act. Without waiting for his commands, she got up and walked to him, listening to her cables sing across the futon. A tinge of fear again: maybe he suspected, maybe the dye was wearing thin, maybe he knew the real thing. But he didn't move, just let her come forward, drop to her knees and breathe on the tent of his pants. "Will you allow me to pleasure you?"

He shook his head and moved past her to sit on the stool. "Come here," he said, patting the fine synthetic of his suit leg.

The tone was just right and the Act reached beyond even

Fields. Like a dancer who knows just the right moves to get from one end of the stage to the other, Fields moved her head just *so* to untangle the trailing decorative umbilicus, a debutante's hair toss, and a step, walking an invisible line to give her hips and bare breasts just enough of a sway. Her lip jutted impertinent and pouty, her hands ran through her nonexistent hair and, instead, tugged a bit on the cables to make sure they didn't grab or snag. Across the room now, in front of the Client now, she stuck a finger under her chin, lowered her eyes and shuffled her feet.

She began to make a noise ("Daddy?") but caught it in her throat at the light in his eyes, the firm tent in his fine pants. The Act had her then, and it had him. His fire and need leaped the gap as she moved closer, putting him into her heat—letting it wash over him.

"Come here," he repeated, patting his knee.

She nodded, her age now lost somewhere between naughty girl and strumpet, and moved toward him, letting the tingling field of his excitement bathe her.

On Daddy's knee, she turned and looked at him. So close, so close, the heat of him—this was his treat, this was what he'd come for. She didn't pretend to know (his hand lifted and traced a fingernail line up the side of her arm and across her left shoulder) what drew them to Autos, but they came. Maybe this was something tight and shut and secret within him, maybe he had suggested the game to someone else and they'd shut it down further so now the only person he could tell this heart to was someone artificial and consciousless. Supposedly.

On Daddy's knee, she arched her back just a bit. One thing they always did come for was the fresh enthusiasm. It was perfect for Fields, she really looked forward to each chance to refine the Act. An Auto would treat each client as if he were the only Client, man, woman, in the world. They matched: the fact of what she was supposed to be, and what she was.

His breath was hot and faster, it warmed the side of her left breast. The nails turned and glided under: her nipple tightened and knotted in front of his eyes. His breath tingled her nipple and she ached to reach around his head and draw his hot and soft (she knew, she knew) mouth to her nipple, to reverse the play and become mother to him. But she resisted, and let she him lead the way.

The hand dropped to her thigh and rested there. She resisted again, trapped in the Act. Fields was in bondage to her performance: Think like the machine, be the machine and let the Act take its way.

I like being the machine, she thought, her mantra as he pushed just a bit against her tight thighs, and she took the cue, spreading them ever just so. *I must be the machine.*

The terror came as he brushed his fingertips up along her slit, tickling the bead of her clit ever just so. The Act: she responded a bit late, a second after the thrill itself, the wave itself, went from pussy to head. A second delay. A second second, and she moaned slightly. She wanted to turn and slip off his leg, turn and face him, spread her legs to let his fine, smooth fingers (nails trimmed professionally short) touch her, explore her. She wanted to be free, but the Act was around her, close and confining. Invisible bondage of acting.

He said something. Something lost in the heat.

"Pardon, sir?"

"Have you been keeping clean?" he said. His voice was constrained and hard, but broke with a crack of excitement. These were his lines, and the fact of it actually happening was taking its toll.

"Yes, Daddy" she said, in tones of slight shame, embarrassment. Resting her hands on her own thighs, she spread her legs a little wider on the balancing Act of his knee.

"All over?"

"Yes, Daddy"

"Even your coochie?"

"Yes, Daddy." *(Machines do not laugh, machines do not laugh, machines do not laugh...you sweet, crazy guy)*

She knew the next: "How did I tell you to do it?" but that didn't stop the tingle when he really did say it. Leaning back into his arm, tucking herself under, she put her head on his shoulder: a silent language *I'm embarrassed.*

He stiffened somewhere else, and she could tell that a wave of shock had made its way through him. His thoughts were almost ringing through her head, too real. The fear made him soften a bit under her leg, made his posture twist. Too real, too real.

Time to bring him back, to let him go. Give him his money's worth: she whispered her adolescent fear into his shoulder again *I'm embarrassed, Daddy* and let him stroke her back, tisk-tisking her into comfort.

"I use a washcloth on my private place," she said, with small hands over her slightly-spread thighs.

It took him a while, coughing it up from his own real embarrassment through his brain via his now-rock-hard cock. "...careful to clean everywhere?"

"Yes, Daddy."

"Especially your pearl."

Quiet, shushed. "Yes, Daddy."

Knew the next line, too, but let it come from him real and quite strong: "Show me how you do it—how I told you to do it."

Dropping her hands into her lap, she spread a bit wider, balancing herself on his knee, leveraging herself on the ridge of his cock. Her clit was a tiny button under her finger, and the first touch was almost too much, too hard and chaffing. The finger went down lower, scooping up a shine of her own juice, and returned to her knot. The first stroke was clumsy and childish, in character: a quick, hard rub up and down with the meat of her hand, pressing up and in. The feeling tore, rather than washed over her. It was a near-kick in the clit. It was too much too hard too soon and she had to use her Act, use the breathing of the machine to keep from making a noise. *State of the Art,* she thought, gripping herself inside to keep from making noise, tightening her thighs too much. *State of the Art—*

"That's it, that's it—" his voice a deep whisper in her ear "—it feels good to clean yourself, doesn't it?"

That was the way she would have started, if she was what he really wanted, so she had given it to him. But that was the Act, that was the realism that he wanted from a machine. Now what he really wanted, what she really fucking wanted: the next stroke was leisurely and circular. She cupped one hand in the other and moved them slow counterclockwise, cupping and working her cunt with her fingers. One thumb stroked and ringed her hardening clit while the other fingers and the other thumb worked into her cunt itself, relishing the muscularity of her, the rings of her muscles, the little no-man's-land between cunt and asshole.

Under her, behind her, Fields felt him tighten, and caught a whiff of the metal tang of his excitement. The gates had been passed, and the Act was running smoothly. A quick jill come climbed up out of her cunt in a series of throbbing quakes. Her legs, her thighs, her tummy jiggled with the coming wave, and she pressed harder and moved faster, and chanced a quick skirt right across the top of her clit.

The orgasm was real—it reached out of her cunt, through her gut, and up her throat in a low moan, finally spilling out of her lips.

Leaning back, she twitched and quaked in his arms. She let herself fall only so far, not making him support her entire weight. Balanced on his leg, she slowly let herself slide down to a crouch on the floor. His hand was on her shoulder, stroking her. His fingernails were lights gliding through her closed eyes. A good performance, a fine come. Act 2:

Turning, she pulled herself now back up, pulling with all her real weight on his pants, climbing the fine suit with clenching hands till she was where she needed to be.

Rubbing the bar in his pants, tracing with her first and little fingers the crown of his circumcised head, she admired it, lost herself in her contemplation of it, getting off on its length (average) and hardness (the Act was really working, it really was). She was working herself up with another hand between her legs (and the sweet slick noise of her cunt juice, and her hard clit swimming in it), and she was feasting on his cock without really touching it.

Sign: his hand gently rested on the back of her head. "Clean Daddy now."

With fluttering skill, she found the zipper and glided it down on its nylon-Teflon teeth. His underwear was peach and also silk. A darker, salty-smelling dot ended at the tent of his ridged crown.

The material was clean, but fragrant with the fine wine of his sweat and the tingle of a few pubic hairs poking through the fine material. She washed it with her tongue, bathing him, tasting the salt of his pre-come. Fields pulled back and admired her work: a darker spread on the fine peach, his cock slowly becoming visible through the damp fabric.

His pants came down. Fingers snaking up, she hooked his belt with one hand, unbuckling with the other. With a hiss of Tokyo tailoring mastery, and the creak from the stool as he stool, they came down.

Dimly, as she pulled down the peach and licked and kissed his hard cock, she was aware of him undressing over her. Tongue around the head, tasting salt and skin. Hands in his short, almost shaved pubic hair, fondling his balls, feeling their wrinkled sack, their bristling hairs.

Too quick, maybe, too sudden probably, but his breathing was quick and deep, his legs were columns of meat and tension.

He slid down her throat, the head rubbing against the ridges of the top of her mouth, the softness, the smoothness of the back of her throat. She swallowed and pulled him close, and kept swallowing him down and down—using those hungry, eating muscles to draw on his cock, milk it, and work it inside her.

Dimly, through all this, she became aware that her other hand was back inside, three fingers deep and working her own reverse throat, playing with the twitching, clenching muscles of her cunt. Her clit was a tight singing, throbbing, pulse between her legs. She soothed it and calmed it and bathed it with a circling thumb, pressing on that special spot just to the right of her slit, hitting her special COME button at just the right instant—

—and somewhere, he was standing over her, his hard, hard, too-hard cock down the back of her throat and she was consuming him, swallowing it down deep—

—and somewhere was the room, somewhere was Fields and her trailing umbilicord prop in a small room in an old factory building in the old, bad part of Kyushu—

—and here was Fields in the Act, connected and linked to this man, this man who came to her, who let down his guard and showed himself to her, and she played with him, and made it real safe and fucking hot. *State of the fucking Art—*

—and he came, a shudder and two hands hard on the back of her head, not pushing, not forcing, just holding himself there. The jets (one, two, three, four—good boy—five, six...) were beyond taste but his body relaxed and oozed the come out of his skin. He broke out in a head-to-toe shine of sweat and giddy release.

Opening wider (was it possible?) she eased him out and kissed and licked him clean, then let her own deep and rumbling come, a thigh-trembling and spine arching (was that her head on the floor, was that his hand on her hand, steadying her, easing her rough ride?) spasm that left her panting almost out of Act, almost to the edge of mumbling "Fucking grand, man—"

Final Act, lady and gentleman: she got to her legs in a supreme Act of control (without a quake, without a mumble, no hand to steady herself) and walked to her private corner of the room.

With the stainless steel bowl of warm water and the soft cloth, she bathed and cleaned his cock and balls. She let him prattle a bit, his *Oh, Gods* and such washing over her. Applause. Applause. *Applause!*

Cleaned, she helped him dress: cocksucking whore to geisha in one quick move. The Act for him was over, the orgasms tasty and filling. The Act, though, was not quite.

Fields showed him to the door, and concluded with a "Thank you, sir. Please come again," in the voice, in the Act. The tones of coolness, not of boredom, but of very, very expensive circuits. A stance slightly stiff, slightly posed, more than slightly mechanical.

She closed the door behind him and stretched out on the futon. The applause of her come, the applause of his come, the applause for the Act. This was someone, and something, she really, really, enjoyed, and could do a really, really long time—

The purr interrupted her quick sleep. Not soon, just long enough for her head to rest.

Mama glowed, a wrinkled goddess with a thin black cigarette, as always, between broken tombstone teeth. In chopped English she woke Fields up—

—and the message worked its way through *("Okay, Mama— okay...")*, "He say he want you—"

"That's great, Mama. I'm broken, though, right? Little Miss Robot busted for the night—"

"No, no, no, he want you. Buy you. He want buy you—"

Fields smiled back at the broken, smiling, teeth. "Good night, Mama."

Applause, applause, applause...

...to sleep.

BLUEBELLE

I see myself sometimes. I don't like it. It's not that I'm ugly; if anything, I'm "utilitarian." It's just that...when I cruise the downtown towers, past the reaching, blown-glass castles of the Acro-cologies, I sometimes catch my reflection in their rippling monomolecular glass. Dark blue, distorted by the organiform architecture, I look even though I don't like the view.

Looking at yourself and seeing that you snore, that you have hairs coming out of your nose, or that you always have to get in the last word—none of us like that, but we always look anyhow. I saw a machine, but I knew that. A globe, the shape dictated by the inversion drive, an imbedded ring making up the scanning gear, the millimeter radar array, the counterinsurgency black boxes, the air-to-airs, the air-to-grounds, the suprasonic crowd suppression stuff, the heavy assault cannon, the 22mm assassination rig, the foam and spasm-gas bomblets. I rarely see myself, but I know what I can do. I'm capable of kicking ass.

I call her Bluebelle. No girlfriend, no old car; no crap like that. When they first strapped me in, I just thought of it. Right out of the, well, what else would you call her? LAPD Enhanced Patrol Unit D-277. She might be a rumbling ball, churning through the stinking air of LA, her inversion drive rippling the smog into oscillating ridges of dark yellow, but she's Bluebelle to me.

5-12 IN ZONE B-3. SUSPECT: CAUCASION, MALE APPROX. 35-40. NIGHTMARE FIST GANG AFFILIATION IDENTIFICATIONS. GET MOVING, ROGER. She's big, blonde, with gold skin. Big

tits. Great ass. Like a racehorse. Man, is she strong. Beat the
crap out of you. But I hold the reins, long, strong leather
strips strung from my gloved hands down to the bit in her
teeth. My saddle is black leather, too, shining like a black
bitch's cheek. My uniform is perfect, as only my Personalized
Command Interface can make it.

Pico and Sepulveda, the smoke from dozens of car fires
turn the night blacker than my saddle, but Bluebelle sees
through it all. First they're dots, then they're glops, then children, then adults, then they become the heat signatures of
citizens, glowing at 98.6 degrees in her infrared eyes. The fires
are there, too, but discounted for their higher temperatures.
She flies down till her nipples hint at scraping on the asphalt,
and I quick-scan for the perp using the low ultraviolet, seek-
ing the telltale fluorescence of Nightmare Fist body work—a
prompt action that gets me a reward. GOOD CALL, ROGER.
THAT SHOULD FLUSH HIM OUT. She turns from her flight to
look back at me, a melting smile on her red-leather plush lips.
Then her hand, lithe and strong as a golden snake, reaches
back between my legs. Her fingers close briefly on my half-
limp cock, warming it, pushing it up my own infrared scale.

Only a small reward, the hand pulls away; the smile
lingers, but not for that much longer. Haven't caught the asshole yet. Dispatch thunders in my ear, the voice of records and
sentence. Again, I disagree with the sentence, but don't argue
with them. I love her too much for that. WE'LL GET HIM, DAR-
LING. THAT'S GOOD ENOUGH.

He glows differently, a pulsing blue against the smoky
darkness, among the fireflies of citizens, between the wire
frames of downtown as seen through her millimeter radar. I
roar as we tear down Pico towards him, a deep-throated battle-
call echoed by her rumbling inversion drive. GET HIM,
DARLING. GET HIM! I know he runs, because they always do, his
image and data growing more complex despite his amplified

muscles trying to get him away. When he flares in front of me I catch the brighter glow surrounding his right hand, something trying to mimic the ultraviolet signature of his tribal skin grafts (a mosaic of dead rivals sealed onto his body) but not accurately. Sloppy work, thank god.

I spur her hard, and we bank right, cutting between a pair of skeletal buildings in the middle stages of growth, frames furry with nanotech in her powerful-zoom eyes. The particle beam makes a sound like loudly tearing paper, its appearance a score across her vision from where the Fist stands to the corner of one of the structures. The nano-grown diamond lattice vanishes in a skyrocket blast of sheared atoms. Again, I bless her speed, her vision, and her bleeding edge counterinsurgency software that kept the Fist from getting a quick and sure lock. FAST THINKING, ROGER! GREAT JOB!

No time for rewards, though. I unholster my pistol, spin the chamber until it gets to meat-seeker. She's seen him, and unless he can shed his skin he's dead.

"Should I, Bluebelle? Should I?"

BLAST HIM, ROGER!

I don't need to aim. That might be my pistol, but between my legs is my gun. Finger on the trigger, my dick is hard. Cock is very hard, pulsing and throbbing. Gloved hand high in the air, I point at a faint sliver of moon and fire. As the shot arcs through the sky, part of her vision the eyesight of the tiny bullet, we pull up until the city is a toy below. WONDERFUL, DARLING, WONDERFUL! She faces me, golden and gorgeous; nipples happy and hard, downy triangle between her legs hot and moist. As the bullet screams down the street, eating up hundreds of feet a second, her hand wraps around my suddenly exposed cock. As the bullet watched the Fist grow bigger and bigger, she took the bit from her mouth and kissed me, her sweet tongue dancing with my own. GREAT JOB, ROGER! As the bullet touches his patchwork chest, she slides her hand up and down my throbbing cock, making me somehow even harder. As the bullet explodes, its precise shockwave turning his chest inside out, painting the building behind him wildly red, she smiles at me.

"Please?" I ask her. "Please, Bluebelle—don't I deserve it?"

Then—bliss—she says, "YES, ROGER; YES YOU DO."

Above LA, my real body long forgotten, she smiled at me golden and gleaming. Her nipples, as red as the carbon monoxide sunset, hardened before my eyes. The downy hair between her legs looked like the polished brass of an old coin. Her lips: no words for her lips because as I was trying to find something around the dying corpse of LA to compare her to she bent down and slowly slid them over my hard, hard cock. No, no words. Sensations, yes, but rationality left as the wet tunnel of her smile dropped down, inch by inch, over me. WONDERFUL, ROGER. YOU DID WONDERFUL!

She had my cock in her mouth and all was right in my world. She said yes, I was being rewarded, and there was nothing better in the whole wide world. Her mouth was the best mouth in the whole world, her tongue the best tongue I'd ever felt. Beyond the plushness of her lips, the delightful firmness of her teeth, it was the giving, my reward. She sucked me, she licked me, she nibbled me—she pulled me up, higher and higher, harder and harder until there was no place else to go but out through hot virtual jism down her insatiable throat.

When I opened my eyes we were above the yellow clouds of the city, and the sun was just starting to warm the horizon.

※

Later, not much later, but later. A few calls between then and now, but nothing that really made my blood pump, that got Bluebelle to even look back at me. We cruised, checking on hot spots for any visible flames; we crawled along the freeways, looking for unauthorized transports; we swept the industrial centers, eyeing green sabotage and illegal dumping. Aside from a few homicides, a few felonies, a few sex crimes, it was quiet.

It started, as it always does. 5-19 IN ZONE A-2. MULTIPLE SUSPECTS. NIGHTMARE FIST GANG AFFILIATIONS. THIS IS IT, ROGER.

We were the closest. Dispatch rumbled the sitrep in my ears, confirmed by her long range eyes. Large building downtown. Doctors' offices. Insurance offices. Municipal offices. 12 perps. 36 hostages. The first demands hacked into the Muninet were for a complete police pullout of Clearlake. LIKE HELL, ROGER.

The canyons of the city opened below me as I dropped down. They swallowed me and soon the roadway again threatened to scrape Bluebelle's nipples. The hot, smog-tainted air swept around me, kicked up by our speed into trailing corkscrews. In her standard vision, the building was a brilliant rectangle among too many other brilliant rectangles, but then it became a wire frame cage containing bright red (hostages) and flickering blue (the Fists). The hostages were on one floor, most of the Fists were on the floor below—only two of them mixing, making a corner of the office a flickering purple. NOT GOOD, DARLING.

Not good was right. I knew SWAT was on the way, knew it as well as my blood pressure, as the number of rounds in my 9mm anti-assault weapons, but I was also first on site. WE GOT TO SCOPE THEM OUT, ROGER.

We boosted, Bluebelle and I, tearing down the office-walled canyon until we could see the infrared-blurred silhouettes of everyone there. We scanned, looking from the basement to the penthouse, searching everything and everyone inside for certain things that didn't belong, things like compressed crystal matrix explosives or tailored mutagenic bacteria. Nothing there, though, but men, guns, and frightened people.

—And millimeter radar tracking weapons. In the saddle, her golden back under me, I felt her long, lean torso tense with the contact of their screaming probes. I saw her muscles clench as they touched then held on. GET THEM OFF ME, ROGER. So I took the reins and pulled her hard and to the left, towards the industrial chaos of a satellite receiving array on top of the Microgyne Building. In a hot second as their weapons fired and the missiles reached us, I took my Bluebelle through the forest of antennas and dishes at close to Mach 1. I watched the micromissiles hit those antennas and dishes, cascades of sparks showering down on us, making her bronze skin shine and shimmer like molten metal. She turned as I turned her back towards the building, smiling up at me, and there I caught the brilliant red of her swollen nipples. Things like that make life worth living.

We leveled off, my hands tight on her reins, the buildings suddenly beneath my feet and skyline in front of my nose. Bluebelle turned then, flipping as only she can do until my saddle rested on her smooth belly, her perfect, big tits in front of me. My reward: she smiled at me, promising kisses and the wonder of her mouth.

LOCK ON, she said as I felt the shimmering contacts on her body. Close. Too close. I knew them without having to look: Australian-made anti-armor, AI-governed, supersonic interceptors. They'd cut through permaplast, they'd cut through reinforced steel, they'd cut through both Bluebelle and I as if we weren't there, and there were three of them behind us. Not close enough to see the marks, MADE IN THE SYDNEY REPUBLIC, but not by much.

ROGER, she screamed, SAVE ME. So I did. I turned, I dove, I twisted, I turned. I brushed her luscious thighs against the sides of downtown architecture (trying for once not to look at us in the glass and ruin the illusion), I skimmed her nipples along the roofs, I nicked her toes on cornices. One exploded into a holographic billboard, sending twists of light into the night; two exploded on a rooftop, tossing up neat octagon chips of nanotech-built carbon with the fireball; and number three hit us in the back.

I don't feel pain. I'm not wired that way. But Bluebelle screamed, a high frequency electronic bellow of agony. Her body under me shimmered and shook as if in a seizure. Her eyes unfocused, she bared her teeth. We dropped quick, smashing off the corner of a rooftop, but my girl is tough and strong. She shook, she sweated, but she kept us from smashing down hard on the pavement. I'M OKAY, ROGER. FLIGHT CAPABILITIES DOWN 21%, DEFENSIVE SYTEMS DOWN 32%, OFFENSIVE SYSTEMS DOWN 10%. LET'S PULL BACK.

I turned her away from the looming black wall of a department store, for a moment our image there in the glass. You have to look; I said that, didn't I? I did, seeing the cold reality of her armor, her systems, the gaping hole in her side, the thin trail of plastic-reeking smoke. Under me she was a goddess, a woman of divine light. Her tits were conical perfection, topped by wrinkled delectation. Her ass was tight, a peach delight. Her cunt was steaming velvet. Her mouth was a hot tunnel of pleasure. She was mine, and I was hers.

I pulled on the reins, turning her hard. In the distance, the building was still lit by status reports and complex graphics from the SWAT teams. Soon it was looming, a geometric Christmas tree of assault percentages, casualty projections, and weapons assessments. I armed the high velocity, multipersonnel rockets. PLEASE, ROGER. PLEASE, ROGER—

I drew my revolver. I didn't need to aim, but I did. With her squirming under me, trying to reach my gun, I still managed to aim. I didn't wait for her to say anything more—I pulled the trigger.

I didn't wait for the explosion. Didn't wait for the casualty reports. I pulled the trigger, sent the explosives on their way, then turned and soared her away from the city.

I had done what needed to be done. I did what I had to do. With the city now rolling far below me, the sirens of the other cops a retreating wail in my ears, I pulled her towards me. She tried to stop me, but I knew she wanted it. I'd done it, after all. I'd done the job.

I forced my tongue in her mouth, dodging her outraged teeth, tasting a slight tang of blood. My hands found her tits, squeezing the soft, sensitive skin between my strong fingers. She hissed, steam escaping from great pressure, and tried to push me away, but I deserved it. My hand found the tangles between her legs and with a quick, deft finger I found soft folds, a pleasurable depth. I fucked with my hand for long minutes—relishing the geometries of her lips, the ring of strong muscle, the smoothness at the deep back of her cunt. I fucked her with my hand, thinking all the time about how it would feel, how it would feel when I—

Hard, I was hard. I was a furious hard. A raging hard. Hard as my pistol. My cock was virtual, but veined—strong, beaded by a drop of righteous come. She tried again to fight, but I was stronger. I'd done my job, and she was mine.

I spread her legs, almost hypnotized by her gleaming, wet folds. My cock, hard—so hard—pulled me forward, demanding to be plunged into her hot, damp depths. But I held back—I held back to simply look at her wet perfection. The ideal cunt. The perfect cunt—and it was mine. I deserved it. It was my reward.

Above that perfect cunt was the flat expanse of her strong belly, the twin plush mountains of her tits and the crimson peaks of her nipples. Seeing her, looking at her spread, wet and sweet, I felt myself become my cock—as if my entire being was crammed into my virtual dick. I couldn't think of anything except fucking her—Bluebelle's cunt became everything

I'd ever wanted.

So...tight, yes; maybe even a bit dry, but soft, tight, and ideal. My cock plunged in and out, back and forth, reaching her depths before drawing back for the fat head to barely emerge. Repeat, repeat, repeat until both my heads—the one between my ears and the one between my legs—swelled and swelled some more, until a scream escaped my lips and come jetted from the head of my cock.

It ended in the hills over the city, both of us hovering lazily high above sick mesquite bushes. She was damaged, the missile having done more harm than either of us thought. It was minutes, when it should have been seconds, for her self-arrest procedures to kick in. Resting, come sticky on my thighs, her restraint foam suddenly boiled onto me, congealing and freezing me into immobility. Outraged, I screamed, I bellowed. I demanded why she should turn on me, arrest me. I cried hot tears as she took control and started us back to base. I wept like a baby as she dropped towards base. Didn't I deserve my reward?

YOU DIDN'T ASK, was all my Bluebelle told me.

WINGED MEMORY

It wasn't easy to find. He'd have been surprised it if had been: "Industry Town, at the end of Press Street. Go to the fence, turn right. Walk between it and the building that smells like fresh lightning till you see the door," the man in the bar had said. A man with hair the color and shape of an explosion, with one eye a steel bearing, twirling a glass of smoky liquor but never drinking.

So: the rust and heavy construction of Industry Town; the narrow way of Press Street; a fence chiming from gusts of hot, dry air; the aroma of ozone (biolight recycling plant); the door—sheet steel with no knob or hinges. He approached and it swung into cool darkness.

Inside, the plastic cocoons of shipping containers: a hall of gigantic orange fingers on fat rubber tires. A gurney from what looked like an ambulance. Coils of cable. A flatscreen monitor on the floor, playing sine waves. Everything was small and portable, easily picked up and carried.

"We have a special today," a man said, stepping out from behind one of the containers, wiping his hands with an oily rag. Moving like an insect in a precise ballet of extraordinarily long arms and legs, he gently folded the rag around a brace ringing one of the containers. His face was long and narrow, pinched and tight; hair the color of old asphalt, the few white streaks of white like pebbles in a road. His names, the man in the bar had said, were many, various. "Someone's collecting virginities. Give you a hundred for losing yours," Various said.

Thinking quick about it, he thought of her, instead: walking the street, eyes available red, steaming lust for rent, the defiant tension in her legs, breasts spilling from the top of a latex dress—creamy crescents under hard streetlight. She offered so much more than what Mary had given him, so many years before.

"More than it's worth to me," Dusk said, stepping closer and smiling.

⁂

After a few minutes—stretching out on the gurney, Various touching the tiny aches of microdermal pickups to his temples—he sold Magnesium Mary and a biting cold March night behind the Autopharm™, for one hundred dollars.

"Think of it," Various said, pulling small tools and loops of floptical cable out of the bright orange industrial jumpsuit he wore, rolled at arms and legs. "Try and remember as much as you can. It'll help."

Dusk watched him move around his head, feeling the connections' pricks and gentle stabs of pain. He didn't want to nod or say anything, so he didn't. After a minute more, Various said "Start" from behind his flatscreen panel—somewhere beyond, above Dusk's head.

Start, *right: a whistling canyon kind of cold, when simply brisk turns snapping, biting from twisting down narrow streets. Sodium lights, he remembered perfectly, crisply—how they made the street look bilious, intestinal yellow. He'd been fifteen, living with Shirley, his mother, in a yellow Datsun next to a Pornotopia store. Already he was running with the Braves but because he was small—he shot up later in life—he didn't get to do much except carry shit. He'd been doing just that, thin nylon shirt packed with Speedex capsules in dirty bubblewrap, when he'd seen Magnesium Mary.*

For a fifteen-year-old she'd been a goddess, a spike-haired bitch queen, dotted with the flashes of steel piercings in eyebrows, nose, lips, and cheeks, who always smoked, always swore, and liked to change her shirt in public to give fifteen-year-olds woodies at the sight of her middle-aged tits and metal-flashing nipples.

It'd been an empty night, the cops having cleared the whole area hours before. It was just Mary, Dusk and the hard concrete behind the Autopharm™. She said something, lost to growing up, but the end of it was her grabbing Dusk by the collar of his windbreaker and hauling him into the sweet-reek of garbage alley behind the pharm. She'd fumbled with his belt, and her words stuck "'bout time you grew up, fuck," as she swallowed his scared-limp dick into her burning mouth.

Her suction drew it out of him in a twenty-second come: spasms of too young muscles plunged into steaming, moist, hotness. He blushed and felt the crashing of humiliation as she stood up and spit his come onto the brick back of the Autopharm™.

His first. Then she slammed her fist into his gut, and while he was puking up a fast-food dinner she ripped the jacket off his back and took all the Speedex caps. When Romeo, the Braves' chief, found out, he beat Dusk some more—eventually breaking three of his ribs.

Take it, man, I don't want it any more, Dusk thought as Various clicked and clacked devices beyond his sight.

After, when the memory had faded, faded, and faded so much that he couldn't answer the musical question How did you lose your virginity? Various unclipped him and told him to get up.

"Be glad you came to me. Someone like Gregorious, you shouldn't trust. I'm much better than he is. I treat you right," Various said, adding finishing touches to Dusk's purchased memory of Magnesium Mary with pianistic gestures across his glowing flatscreen. After a tattoo of his long, thin (and, Dusk noted absently, pink-painted nails) fingers he held up a tiny wafer of dull silver. "Lost virginity on a chip," he said, then took Dusk's debit card, paid him his hundred, and sent him away.

Fifty went to back rent. It felt good, but not great, to spend some of his hundred putting off getting kicked out by another month, a little towards his debt. It felt so good, in fact, that he blew another ten getting the lights turned back on in his rack box. There was a rare satisfaction, as he swiped his card through the manager terminal in the lobby, that for what seemed like months he wouldn't have to sit in a black box. Now, for ten Revalued dollars, he could have lights for a month.

Then Dusk walked the length of Cancer Alley for three hours.

Sometime in the past, Dusk had been told, you could see the sky. Now though, the Alley pinched upwards—buildings on both sides built up generation over generation, shanty on vertical shanty—till there was nothing but cardboard, plywood, plastic truck cocoons and cheap-ass capsule hotels and no sky, never, ever.

There were stars, though. Illiterate Dusk navigated by a thousand flickers from shorting, chopped power lines and greasy cooking fires.

Cancer Alley wasn't that long—just three miles from old St. Fluke hospital (one end) to the New Deal Toxic Recycling Facility (the other) — but Dusk hadn't seen her yet, so he just walked from one end to the other. It took him three hours of walking from the ghost of the old public hospital to the sound of screaming, breaking carcinogens to find her.

He'd seen her before, of course, walking up and down this narrow stretch, proudly offering her charms. Dusk had been struck by her, an electric and full-voltage attraction the first time he'd seen her but then, walking in the always-twilight of the alley, he was hard pressed to say why, and what, exactly, she looked like.

Then she was there and he was ... surprised by her. He didn't know why, but he was. He also didn't know why being surprised would make him stop for a second and just stare at her as if he was seeing her for the first time.

Which, he knew, he wasn't.

Big eyes, full of available red. She was pure lust—excitement—for rent. Her legs were packed with muscle and defiant tension, covered with the high, reflective gloss of thick latex. Nasty three-inch heels. Her hair was smoke, a curly mass of black, drifting strands that surrounded her elegant face like a storm cloud wrapping a strong mountain peak. Her breasts were cream, big and full, pressed in a many-buckled shiny latex top.

She looked at him and turned, not picking Dusk out of the crowd, not noticing him since he didn't appear to have money. Her back was naked, save for the lashings of her top, to the fine dip of her coccyx. On her back, the tattoo of a single wing. It was so shaded, so realized, that Dusk had to look twice to make sure it was ink in skin, and not something else.

Not knowing what kind of self-protection software she might be running in addition to her whoreware, Dusk didn't do what he wanted to—which was to tap her on her strong shoulder. Instead he stepped behind her and cleared his throat.

"Yeah?" she said, voice rumbling with caution.

Dusk held up his debit card.

She took it, slid it through the narrow plastic slot on the checker bracelet on her left wrist. Her eyes went from red to green. Sufficient credit. Thirty minutes of her was his.

"This way, lover," she said, now with tones of warmth, of moisture, of heat.

This way was into the lobby of a once grand, but now sad and frightening hotel. Its name was long gone, and even the ghostly pattern of where the lettering had been was scrubbed clean. Three flights, past three extended families living on two floors and in one hall, and then a door. 313. She slid her thumb down the jamb and a solid bolt slammed back.

The room was sparsely furnished: black futon on industrial rubber floor, yellow and black halogen work lamp, a bright red plastic toolbox, and a large suitcase.

She turned and smiled, a beam of pure kindness. "Make yourself comfortable, darlin'." Dusk sat down and kicked off his shoes as she walked with fluid temptation over to the tool-box and rummaged its contents. His socks (holes in both) went into his shoes as he watched her, trying to freeze the beauty of her actions in his mind. Standing, he pulled off his shirt, dropped it next to his shoes. Then belt, pants, underwear.

Naked, he stood. The room wasn't cold but he shivered anyway.

She turned, smiling comedy and lust at his hard cock. "Lie down," she said, motioning to the futon with a quick move of her head.

Dusk did, moving this way and that on the lumpy surface till it felt reasonably comfortable. He noticed, absently, a huge yellow water stain on the ceiling, a curious parade of lights from something reflective on the street below. She walked, all elegance and steam, to stand next to his head. His eyes followed the fine geometry of her legs up till they reached the shadowy mystery hidden by her dress.

With a nice move, she put one foot on either side of his head, facing towards his feet. Even with the dancing lights on the ceiling, he couldn't see anything but soft shadows between her legs.

"Don't blink or you might miss me," she said, and a flash of pure, white light licked up one side of her left leg and showed him (blink, blink) the pale curves of her ass, the cream contours of her mons, the gentle folds of her majora—then it was gone and there were shadows again.

She moved a bit more, and again the light flashed, and again Dusk was teased with a burst of white skin blending to pink, of gleaming moisture, of an outer opening *just so*. Darkness—

He realized that she had a small light in one hand, was using it to draw back the shaded curtain of her dress, showing herself with quick flips of the flashlight. Then he wished he hadn't understood the trick—magic explained is a little less magical.

The light again, and this time he caught the butterfly flicker of her hand, and he saw something, in addition: blood-red nails on lovely frosty-white fingers covering her mons, cupping herself.

The next beat, the next pass, the light stayed—lingering on the sight of her hand between her legs, her brilliant red nails. As he watched, (not blinking, not ever) the fingers moved, a massaging ballet on her obscured cunt. His imagination got up and ran fast and far away, and he dreamed an impossible view between red-painted nails and the churning, melting folds of her. He saw, but couldn't really have, her fingers stroke and tap the big pearl of her clit, press up and part her very pink and glistening lips.

Then, he did. Really. She parted her fingers and showed him, opening herself far above him, drawing back her majora to feast him on the sight of her hot, wet inner self. Her clit was big, like one of her own red-painted nails. Her lips were fat and puffy, and her color sunset red.

His hand found his iron cock, closed around it. He was there, holding his aching self for just a throb (two?) of his pulse—long enough to feel it in a strong vein—then she said, strong but firm: "No, no—save it."

Turning, she smiled (humor, delight, steam) and carefully lowered herself down, her arms out like a laughing gymnast, and guided the flowered opening of her cunt over his nodding cock till her lips met and kissed his head. She stayed here, letting him gently tap and stroke her lips with his throbbing dick.

"Suck me?" he asked, his voice so soft and weak it scared him.

She shook her head, hair floating in the warm air. "Sorry, lover—don't do that."

She continued to rub herself, allowing him to feel the contours of her cunt with his cock head till the ache in his balls started to change, started to build. The muscles in his back, chest and groin felt knotted, bound up with a pounding tension—yet all of his attention was focused on the subtle feelings of his screaming cock head gliding over her moist folds, gently gliding past her wet cunt. He wanted to reach up and pull her down and himself into her but he held back, grabbing coarse handfuls of the futon. The torture was ecstasy.

Then she did it. With that balletic, gymnastic skill she scooped up his cock with her cunt mouth and pushed him up inside her with one long hot stroke. He almost came right then and there, for some reason he was able to reach down inside himself and still the straining urge.

Slowly, she withdrew again till his head again was out in the warm air, then she pushed herself onto him again. Like that, in and out—all the way in (tap cervix) all the way out (warm air). His balls went from just yelling to maniacal screaming. His back went from knots to pulsing waves of agony. His cock felt bigger than he was, taking up all of his feelings and nerves (his hands, fanatically clutching the futon, were as far away as the moon) as she slid it in and out of herself.

She had been looking down at his chest, concentrating on the dance she was giving his cock, but after a short while she looked up at him, locking her glowing green—*paid*—eyes at him. Smiling, she arched her back and carefully (expensive) reached down and flipped the top of her dress down, giving him a view of her breasts, the soft slopes of her tits dotted by large, crimson nipples.

He watched her fuck him, her big (but surprisingly not too big) tits gently lifting and falling, heavy and firm, as she did so. He watched and got lost in the feeling of her, the sight of her (green eyes).

Then, when he felt the pressure build so much that it felt far too fucking good to hold it back any longer—he came.

When his heart slowed down enough, when his legs unknotted, when he pried his claws off the bunched fabric of the futon and he could breathe without wheezing, he regained his eyesight: she had taken a little packet of medicated wipes and gently cleaned off his dick and balls. Then she helped him get up and into his clothes.

In the hall, he cleared his throat, asked her name.

"Wing," she said, tapping one shoulder, meaning her back, the tattoo. Then her eyes CLICKED red, his time was up, the sale concluded, and she said, "Get the fuck away from me, dickhead."

❋

Some time must have passed. He was sure of it, almost positive. Dusk would have liked to have had some pause, the knowledge that he hadn't simply stumbled downstairs and run across town. Industry town, chain-link, ozone, Various—

But, after, he didn't really know. When he was up he knew he must have waited at least a week, a few days. When depressed, he knew—deep down and solid—that he had run there, without even waiting a handful of seconds.

Some things had stayed. He didn't know, couldn't tell you if you asked, how he'd lost his virginity. He remembered his second time, a hooker his older brother—on leave from the war—had paid for, but he knew that wasn't the first. He remembered being scared and ashamed. But for what and why there was just a hole, an ache with no context.

But Various was crystal clear: hatchet face, piebald hair, odd accent. Legs and arms that looked stretched, too long for his body. Painted nails. He remembered the smile on his face, too, when the door opened and Dusk walked in. It was a broad and toothy smile, a *pleased to see you* smile but with a hard tinge that said he wasn't really interested in Dusk, only the *you* that meant client, customer, *cash.*

"So glad you're back," he'd said, taking Dusk's hand and shaking it once. "So glad—thought maybe you'd gone over to that hackworker Gregorious. So what are you here to sell me today?"

Dusk hadn't smiled, didn't move. He'd stood, stock-still, trying to be iron and resolute, in charge of himself and the situation: "What're you buying?"

But Various had laughed a wheezing, rasping laugh and his black, bushy eyebrows danced like a cartoon character's. "Me? I buy everything! Ask around! They'll tell you that I take whatever's around—you got it, I'll buy it."

"Fine," Dusk said, trying to relax by leaning back against one of the containers, crossing his arms.

"Got a special today. Want to sell your fifth birthday?"

For Dusk, birthdays had never been "special"; the only reason he even knew his was because it was the last six digits on the indenticode tattooed on the inside of his left calf. Somewhere though, when he was ten, he'd seen a vid or an advert or something that mentioned the concept of a birthday. He'd crawled from his bed in the front seat of the Datsun to ask Shirley about it. Maybe luckily, maybe not, she'd been straight enough to answer him: "Gave you that, damnit" she'd said, meaning the indenticode—his name, genetic code, identity registered with the gov. "No one's gonna snatch and sell you if you have that. So what else you want?"

Later, when he'd been big enough to split and not look back, he'd gotten busted for selling Squeak. They'd scanned the indenticode, trying to find a match to his genetic profile, check his record for being runaway, or a parole violator. The little scanner had farted an off-key bleep. "Fucker's fake," one of the cops had said of the tattoo, laughing. "No records, no match."

After thirty days in a crowded lockdown, a listing container ship in the harbor, Dusk had walked through three different kinds of bad neighborhood to find the Datsun burnt and his mother, gone.

Dusk got down on the cot, closed his eyes: "Take it."

❋

Fifty went to his landlord. Dusk watched, smiling, as he inched his way slowly toward black on the lobby monitor. A ways to go, but at least not as far behind as he'd been before.

At least Dusk thought so—he couldn't remember exactly how much he'd owed.

It took him a while to find his coffin, they all looked alike. Luckily he was able to decipher the half-worn-off marks on his key card and find his room of the last three years.

There he stretched out, staring at the ceiling of his capsule, trying to fathom why the pattern of stains around the broken entertainment system looked so new, so unfamiliar. After a time, as his eyes stared to droop, he tried to find the empty memory—trying to explore it like a missing tooth, working himself around the hole it had left. But he couldn't find anything: it was intangible against other yawning holes, other fragments and broken pieces.

Eventually his confusions faded in his tired mind and Dusk slept; if he dreamed he didn't remember that either.

※

The street had a name, but Dusk couldn't read. The signs that flickered and floated, flashed and pulsed were just colored lights to him. It didn't matter, he was following something as intangible as their holographic displays, a fraction of memory, a series of his own hovering images: red eyes, smoky hair, red hooker's eyes, a single wing on a marble back. He knew he felt something for her (the strength in his cock and a pain somewhere in his chest) but the contexts, the pillars of it all, were rotten with holes. He knew he felt something for her— whatever her name was—but he'd be damned if he knew why or for how long.

Then he saw her, and some of it came surging back up into his consciousness: warmth, lust, affection, kindness—he was battered with a rainbow of feelings that, without memories to anchor them, tipped him, drunken and disoriented. Almost falling, Dusk stumbled into a leper ("Back off, freak!" the leper had said, or tried to say, his jaw held in place with duct tape, as Dusk stumbled on) and managed to cross the street.

She stood with a tiny knot of other rentable women, recognizable because of her carriage (proud and strong), her attitude (cool and examining), and her back—which was turned towards Dusk, showing him the graphic of her name, her icon—though Dusk couldn't remember what it was, exactly.

Sensing his approach, she turned, locking him with her brilliant red FOR HIRE eyes. "What you want, fuckface?" she snarled, hand on latex hip, eyebrows knitting hostility at his dazed face, unsteady walk.

Dusk held up his debtcard. She swiped it, coolly and professionally, and her eyes CLICKED emerald.

Her smile in the forever shadows of Cancer Alley was a beam of pure benevolence—as long as his credit lasted. "Are you okay, lover?" she said, taking his arm and steering him towards an ancient building, "Took the wrong kind of candy?"

"I can't remember," he said, honestly, allowing himself to be towed along, into the ruinous cavern of a hotel.

✳

She showed him her pussy, flashing it at him with the clicks of a tiny penlight. Sprawled under her, he watched, enraptured, as she flipped its detail-enhancing whiteness over her plush lips, her folds, and the tiny head of her crimson clit. His cock ached for a touch, any touch, even his own—but she forbade that, telling him to "save it up" with a firm, yet kind, voice.

"Suck me?" he asked, feeling childish and small, towered over by her strength and power.

She smiled, bent over and kissed him, lightly, on the tip of his nose. "I don't do that lover. But I have some other tricks up my—well, you'll have to see, won't you?"

Standing again, she carefully reached into the top of her latex dress and scooped out two handfuls of pale breast, topped by angry red nipples. Then she hovered above him, smiling down at him with feral lust, her cunt a foot, maybe two, away from his face and her heavy breasts above him, eclipsing the too-hard light thrown from the halogen work lamp. Looking up, he could see her nipples; large, red, tasty— *tasty* because she lowered herself slowly down till she squatted over his bare chest, dipped them towards his mouth. "The right one first," she said, and he did: pulling it into his mouth, licking and sucking (gently at first then with greater vacuum). She responded, arching herself backwards and hissing like some kind of pressure was escaping.

"Now the other," she said, repeating the performance. Her nipple filled Dusk's mouth, getting harder and harder and bigger and bigger till he had the sudden desire to full his mouth with it, to suck her whole tit. He tried and she moaned, a deep animal sound, as she rubbed her cunt on his hairy chest.

"Enough," she giggled, standing, "you'll make me come." Turning, she lifted what little of her latex hadn't already been lifted, showing him the perfect globes of her ass, the strength in her towering thighs. As he watched, hypnotized by his throbbing cock and need, she slipped two quick fingers down to her cunt, spread her lips, and briskly circled her clit a few dozen times, moaning all the while.

"Please," slipped out of his lips, soft and small but she heard anyway. Turning yet again, she hovered herself over his bobbing, straining cock. Then, with a skill that summoned memories in him, she started to lower herself down onto him.

Memories cascaded through Dusk's fevered mind, an avalanche of sensation, emotion: *the grasp of her wet cunt as she slid over his cock, the snapshot of her face as she lowered herself down into him, the rocket of orgasm as he jetted into her—the smile on her face as he did.* Though fragments, they still had power. Even before she managed to get his cock into her, he came: an aching, quivering come, and spurted cream into the folds of her cunt, still inches from even touching his cock.

She smiled and, to him, it was kind of sad. With expert moves, she cleaned his cock and herself before waiting patiently for him to get dressed.

In the hall, the door shutting behind him, he reached out of his depression, the hot blanket of sadness that was around his shoulders, and asked for her name.

"Oh, sweetie," she said, touching his nose with an elegant finger, "I told you before." Then her eyes CLICKED to red and she turned and walked off, never looking back.

✳

Things were gone, had been taken, their absence was obvious—how Dusk felt, what he saw inside himself didn't add up to what his age should have been according to his indenticode. He felt nine, ten—not thirty-eight. He didn't have the memories of someone that old.

He sat, quiet and still, on a street he didn't know, watching people walk by that he felt he should know but he simply...didn't.

Some things remained, but just enough to hurt—Dusk remembered the smell of his first home, the yellow Datsun (pine and the peach airspray his mother used) but he couldn't remember where it had been and when he'd seen it last. He remembered what job he'd had before being laid off (bioengine repair) but could barely remember what a bioengine looked like or needed to get fixed. He knew how the scar on the back of his hand got there (beaten by the cops after getting caught for dealing Squeak), but if you'd asked him (then and there) he wouldn't have been able to tell you when that was and how old he'd been.

Dusk didn't even know where he lived. He knew what it

smelled like, what his room number was (201) but he didn't know if it was near or far—that part of his key card was worn away. He knew he owed some back rent, though—but how much was a mystery.

Some things were solid, yes, but it all floated on guesses, suppositions, and doubt.

Dusk knew, for instance, that he had wanted to come here, to the shadowy world where the buildings met high overhead and a thousand small fires created the illusion of ... stars? He felt it, like a firm hand holding his stomach, there was something important here, something that he wanted more than anything. He knew that it must cost, too, because he had a debit card with a hundred on it.

He sat and watched, feeling the cool air from the far end of the street play around his ankles, chilling him. He sat and watched, taking it all in like he was drowning, trying to fill the gaps in his memory with new things: a dwarf with brilliantly-polished chrome legs selling a vat-fed catfish (on a soy bun) from a pushcart; an elegantly elongated black man who towered seven-plus over the crowd, coolly checking the time on an antique gold watch surgically set into his palm; a brilliantly red woman, a flesh and bone clichéd demoness, who leaned into the window of a plush and immaculate pocket racer and danced her muscular ass as she bargained with the driver; a wilding of rogue schoolchildren, still in the threadbare remains of their Catholic uniforms, flowing by and over a massively swollen derelict—when they had passed Dusk noticed they had neatly stolen the bum's prosthetic eyes.

Dusk drank it in, trying to find something, anything, that had meant something to him.

A trio of women, the newest generation of the oldest profession, stood on one corner: a large black woman, her hair a torrent of braids; a mixed-blood lanky one in a tiger-striped poncho; and a pale amazon, breasts all but spilling from the top of a black latex dress.

She turned away, her eyes skipping and glancing off Dusk and the Rent-a-Bench™ he sat on as she turned. Her back, he saw—he stared at—was bare and marble white save for a tremendous tattoo of a single bird's wing.

Dusk watched her, trying to understand his feelings—why he should feel a weight of sadness, a powerful tug of desire, and the soft prickling of infatuation for her. But the feelings were faint, lost without their context. He stood, thinking of approaching her, offering his fat debit card, trying to recapture what she must have meant to him. No, what she must have meant to *him*—the other Dusk who remembered.

The fury built and seemed to break him apart inside—he wanted to get up and scream, start punching. He wanted *something* painfully, totally—the thing that had given him the most pleasure in...he couldn't remember when. He wanted that hope and peace.

It had been something to do with her, he was sure. But he didn't know what.

After an hour of watching her, of feeling the pain at not knowing what to do, how to do it, or why, he got up and retraced his footsteps, stringing together a handful of memories that slowly led him backwards.

✳

Two stops first. One at a small shop he stumbled across, something in its front window grabbing his attention and holding it. He went in and bought the thing, hoping he knew how to make it work.

Then, a name—just that. But names had faces, had bodies. Dusk went to three different bars till he was able to say *that* name and have someone nod up and down. They knew of him, yes. They knew what he did, yes. They knew where he lived, yes.

After, with his purchase—and his new sale completed—he

let his feet lead him the rest of the way backwards through what memories remained to him.

It was easy to find. His feet knew the way, some kind of deep, instinctual repetition. He let them take him to Industry Town (the smoke and hot metal smell of it), then to the end of Press Street. He went to the fence and turned right. The smell of ozone. The door—no handles.

It opened when he approached. The inside was familiar—and the strangeness of that feeling (of knowing) gave him a burst of strength.

"Ah, back so soon?" the man said, stepped out from behind one of the huge orange containers. "I'm glad. Always good doing business with you."

Dusk smiled as the door closed behind him. When it shut, he pulled out the gun and leveled it at the man—whose name he did not know.

The man froze, fear widening his eyes, clenching his teeth. He seemed on the verge, just about, to make light of it, to try and depressurize Dusk and his gun—but then he stopped, held back by the coolness, the unwavering precision of Dusk's movements.

Stepping closer, Dusk cocked the gun and pushed the weight of it into Various's belly; Shoving hard, smelling fear on the man's panting, quaking breath, Dusk felt for Various's lower rib with the muzzle.

Pinned to the wall, his eyes hunted but found only Dusk's marble face, his level breathing, his unbending arms, the ache of the gun's barrel—warmer than Dusk by far.

"*Mercy,*" Various whispered, the word broken and hoarse.

Dusk echoed the word: "Funny—saw someone about that. You know him. Gregorious. Bought it all."

Watching, trapped, he saw Dusk reach into a pocket, pull out something small, silver, silicon.

"Mercy?" Dusk offered, smiling coldly.

EULOGY

It would have been too rude to just not answer the phone for, say, a few years. Ignore email. Not answer the door. I didn't want to, but I had to see her eventually.

It had been three months, and her eyes were still swollen. "Hi," she said, standing at the door, shoulders covered by a bright blue kinetic reflection cape. I was glad to see it. My neighborhood ate its dead, and killed its living. I would have felt so much worse having to worry about her getting in, and eventually out, alive.

"Oh, Julie," I heard myself say. But then nothing else could come. In the end, I resorted to "Come in, come in." That's me, always there with a quick, appropriate witticism. No, normally that was me, but right then the only thing I could come up with was tears.

Julie was never a big girl; she had this...well, narrow presence. Lithe, like a sudden whisper in the middle of a conversation. There: I couldn't have been that upset. "Sudden whisper in the middle of a conversation," that was more like the real Jeff Hook. Worldnet journalist, unsuccessful on-line novelist, and dweller in a scummy part of town.

Well, now that I knew that seeing Julie hadn't upset me enough to jar me from my essential "Jeff Hook"-ness, I could continue. Julie was even less of a whisper, more like just a hint of a woman: she'd been hollowed out, leaving behind just the skin of her life.

I sat her down and made her some soy tea. The cup in her hands, she stared down into the dark steam. "Oh, Jeff. I miss him so much."

Sitting down next to her, I put my arm around fragile shoulders, pulled her closer. "We all do, babe. We all do."

Her hand stroked my leg. I didn't know what to think or do, so I just held her. "Do you remember that time in Venice? When we got so drunk?"

Always one of my favorite things, my friends first remembering me when I was crocked. Still, it did make me smile. "Oh, yeah; oh, yeah. What was it, plum wine? Tom had just finished that big restoration thing down by the Lido. I remember standing there as he explained all this weird science stuff about forced geometries and inversion fields. I got it all for an article but didn't understand a word of it."

She pushed herself upright, suddenly struck by a bolt of life. "No, we got really drunk later. We were celebrating the thing, and got to drinking that hideous Italian stuff—not plum, silly, that's Japanese—but it was really awful, then he took us back out there onto the jetty. I remember standing there, looking at this shimmering wall of water, just hanging there."

I nodded, her excitement grabbing my guts and twisting. "Creeped me out. The thought of all that just hovering there, waiting for the wrong mathematical...something to go wrong and splat! there we and the city go: ketchup in a glass of water."

She frowned and the pain took a sharp plunge downward. "It was scary, but also beautiful. Do you remember what he did? He stood there, facing us, his arms out like this, like he was taking a grand bow or something, and he just stepped back into that wall of shimmering water until he was half in and half out. It was wonderful. I was scared, Jeff, but it was more beautiful than anything I'd ever seen."

I remembered it, too, remembered the expression on Tom's face as he stood there: Moses bathed in the waters. Sometimes, though, when I remembered it, it wasn't the three of us there on that sandy islet, it was just Tom and I, the waters roaring over his tightly muscled body, his cock like Moses' staff in his hand.

"So like him," Julie was saying, her hand still on my leg. "He was like a little kid sometimes. Remember when he got that contract to work with Veloski on that atmospheric bells project?"

Veloski had been a temperamental jerk, this massive Russian bear with all the bad habits of a sweater queen. Nothing was good enough for him. Not the Worldnet coverage (me), not the Field Projection Technician (Tom) or his girlfriend (Julie). The Project was housed in an old cathedral, gutted after the Vatican collapse of twelve years before, and I can still hear his rumbling voice as he condemned the equipment for being shoddy (Tom), the all-prodding media (me), and various hangers-on (Julie). If God hadn't been burned with the rest of Vatican I would have sworn that Veloski was an Old Testament father figure cheesed off that someone had jerked off or something.

Julie and I had hid in the media truck, crouching there with the rest of the hacks and technicians, trying to smile in our foxhole while we knew Tom was being crushed and crushed again by the thunder-on-the-mountaintop ego of Veloski. That was the first time I'd hugged Julie. In our humming, ozone-smelling foxhole we'd held each other and tried to lamely giggle over the poor translation of a Chinese gangster movie that was flickering on one of the truck's constellation of monitors.

I wish I could say that I was overcome by a sudden attack of bravery, but the truth is I was summoned by the man himself. At first I thought that I'd been deserted by Julie, that there'd be nothing between me and a Russian cock ready for reaming, but as I walked through the burnt and warped cathedral doors I felt her hand, a ghost of a gesture, on my shoulder.

No Russian—just the vast empty space—and the sound. I'd

never heard anything like it before, and haven't heard anything like it since. It wasn't even really like a sound, but that's the closest thing I could think of at the time. It was more like something I felt, as if my bones were strings and the vibrations moving through that old, dark church were an invisible bow.

"He was so proud, Jeff. He just stood there, beaming at us. With that...sound, or whatever it was, ringing and ringing. Just standing there, smiling. Wasn't I crying?"

Julie hadn't been the only one. Having had artistic and technological differences, Veloski had stormed off, leaving Tom, "an imaginatively crippled engineer", to fiddle with the great machines until in a burst of inspiration he'd accomplished what the moody Russian never could.

Julie leaned against me, her breath warming my shoulder. "He didn't do it often, but sometimes he'd get his gear out and do it again for us."

"I always wanted him to record it, to share it." I laughed. "And he always said that he didn't want to. Wanted it to just be ours."

"I loved him so much," Julie said. "Why did he have to go?"

I shrugged. "It happens, Julie. Not that often, but it still does. He just happened to get hold of one of the really bad ones. Could have caught it anywhere. He went everywhere, you know."

She kissed me, then. She just tilted her head and then leaned forward, placing her warm, thin lips against mine. At first, I didn't do anything but feel her warmth against me, her soft skin against my soft skin. But then she pushed herself further forward, harder against me. She opened her mouth and so did I, breathing each other's hot breaths. I absently wondered if she could smell that I'd had pizza for dinner.

Then her tongue touched mine. The shock wasn't electric; that's the stuff of romance, or bad porn. No, it was better than electric. It was deep and hard. Our tongues fit perfectly together, muscle against muscle. Heat added to heat. Deep and hard. Our breaths synchronized, and we steamed together like a pair of heavy engines.

"Remember that rainy day in July? I don't remember the year, but it was July. I know it was July. Fireworks at night in a summer sky. We'd had dinner, just you and I, Tom far away somewhere, playing with his great invisible sheets of power. Just you and I. You wanted it, too. I could tell. I really could. I wanted it too, you know, I wanted it just as bad.

"But we didn't do it. No, we loved him too much to do that—or maybe we were just cowards."

Julie's hand on my thigh, fingers around my denim-covered cock. How I'd wanted her hand there that July. Having it there now...I bucked gently against her, fucking her hand through my pants as we kissed and kissed and kissed.

We stopped to breathe air that wasn't from each other's mouths. Julie smiled at me, a smile I'd never seen before. Her eyes were still puffy, her cheeks still sunken, but there was a glimmering in her pale brown eyes. I knew Julie laughing, I knew her angry, I knew her mischievous, but I realized that this was Julie looking up after being dragged down somewhere deep.

I didn't fight her as she pulled my jeans down. "Thank you, Jeff. Thank you." My shorts were very everyday, too everyday for a blow job from a love of my life, but that was only one of many thoughts humming through the cavern of my mind. "I never got to say good-bye, you know." She had my cock in her hand; still through material, but this time the thinner cotton of my shorts. She stroked me, staring up into my eyes. "Thank you. Thank you so much."

Then my cock was out, free in the air. Her hand was so soft. We kissed again, as she stroked me. Time stopped as she performed an action I'd dreamed about for years. Fantasy and reality clashed in a hammering of my heart: each beat seemed to slip between what Julie was really doing versus the countless times I'd stroked myself, and dreamed. Quickly, though, reality took over the total hammering of my pump and it was just me, Julie, and my cock.

Then, quickly—so quickly that I actually caught my breath deep in my lungs—it was Julie's mouth and my cock. Hot, wet, silk, the tightness of her throat, the tiny terrors of just enough teeth. She worked oral magic on me. I leaned back, jutting my hips forward, lost in the feeling of her lips, tongue, throat.

Then she stopped, saying in a soft voice, "Thank you, thank you. Tom would have wanted us to be happy." Laughing: "I think it's a great eulogy."

I pushed her away, put my cock back in my shorts. "Ambrose Bierce."

She frowned, looked about to cry. She might have said "What?" or might have just started to cry. I can't remember. I do know I finished the joke: "A saint is a sinner, revised and edited."

I pulled her head up, looked in those dark-ringed eyes. "Remember that time in New York?"

She didn't want to, but she nodded.

Tom had been involved in a new field project, part of an archeological dig to get a good look at the bottom of the Hudson, except this time he didn't have a Veloski to play the foil. Professor Cohn had been old, pragmatic, and only interested in seeing what mysteries lay at the bottom of the muddy river. Time had been critical, since the city could only stop river traffic for three days.

Two of those days were wasted by Tom playing with new sounds and tricks with his field generators. Then one day became just six hours. Six hours to part the water and show miracles: generations of priceless debris, hundreds of years of waterlogged history. In the end six hours were barely enough time to look, let alone reclaim. The university sponsoring the project tried to get additional funding, but Cohn died two months later.

"He only wanted to play. Like a big kid. But he hurt that professor, for no damned good reason." She blinked, slow and steady. I could see that she was hurt, but she had to be hurt more. That's all there was to it.

"Remember LA?" That should do it. Feel the knife go in, feel it turn. Julie and Tom were together a lot, but not always. Their jobs and Tom's need to play with his invisible toys kept them apart for months at a time, but they still considered themselves a couple. I know, old-fashioned nonsense, but there you go. Old-fashioned for Julie, at least. LA was just the one she found out about, but once she'd found the evidence, discovered what to look for, the others were obvious.

Tom hadn't denied it; I give him that at least. But he didn't stop, either. Gave her some lame excuse about needing to explore life, needing to experience as much as possible. He didn't stop, she just learned to look the other way.

I kissed her again, but it was a quick, chaste kiss. I had to make this good; screw it up and I'd be right back in the jaws of death. "If you want to, then I want to. But if you want to do something for him, then remember him and our times with him for what they really were, and who he really was—not what you want him to be."

We talked for a while after that, a little about the dear departed Tom but also about stupid, miscellaneous stuff. When it got late enough for both of us to start yawning, I called a cab and saw her safely away.

✳

I hated myself. I hated myself for so many things, but was finally able to sleep in the end because it had only been a quick contact of lips on cock.

We have to honor the dead in our own way. I just didn't

want Julie to honor a lie. I loved Tom, loved him in many ways and for many years, but he wasn't worth dying for; well, wasn't worth Julie dying for.

You can't catch it easily, but I managed. At least I got it from someone I loved.

My own eulogy would be a lot simpler: I'd be honoring him soon enough. And, as opposed to Julie, I might be able to ask him if he liked it.

BUTTERFLIES$

—*really was in the rocking, steel-plated guts of a 4-Sale-4-Cheap super-tanker somewhere off in the Sea of Japan, really in that seasick haven for maverick outlaw programmers, really was in a second-skin complex polymer suit packed with the best-you-can buy state-of-the-art neurofacilitators, really was jacked into the public domain Glade of the Datasea—*

No, just kidding, Cole was really *virtually* in a too-beautiful scene: walking through too-green parkland, on picture-perfect grass, under a too-blue perfectly perfect sky—

—and a butterfly was flirting with her.

COME WITH ME, FOREST QUEEN the butterfly flashed with dosed-Disney wings—zooming rudely, filling her field of vision, becoming a sprite with wings, with a leer and smile the size of a house. Back when the gear still smelled of packing she might've whipped the set off her face and panted with shock—now she absently noted that the butterfly's face was artful, elegantly programmed.

OH, PRETTY LADY said yet another, fluttering up from nowhere, flashing Technicolor words at her. I KNOW WHAT YOU WANT, another. A faster flicker of brilliant wings, and then there were two hundred—a fission done with programming cubism. LET ME MAKE SWEET TO YOU—just how many were there? Cole saw nothing but the strobes of fractal wings, heard nothing but soft applause. Laying on her bunk in the creaking, groaning, oil-smelling, too-small cabin on the Liberty ship, Cole was *really* in her suit, *really* rolling on deep sea waves—and was *virtually* being assaulted by a mad swarm of—for god's sake—*butterflies*.

They were nothing, *really*, but a feeling of electric soft-ness, and the sharp spice of almost pain. Assault, okay, but is it rape when you can click your heels together—and be back in Kansas? O-U-T in VRslang and she would be back to the main menu, and out of the satellite link. Besides, she had some pretty snazzy Security and immune-system software. What could happen?

Like a great 256 color wave the swarm...swallowed her. It was like falling, splashing, into an ocean of small, brilliantly beautiful colors and the feel of silk and bristle-brushes. She was lifted and carried into a zero-G oasis of a thousand silken wings, a million miniature hands, a billion tiny cocks. Zooming, one of the swarm, one of the gang, filled her eyes with naked elfin body, a long and hardening cock, and then nothing but a slyly smirking face.

Oh, he, she, *they*—were good, Very good.

The wings were eyelashes batting at her breasts, tickling her ass, flickering their gentle edges across her stiffening nipples, brushing the brush and thicket of her pussy, the pad of her mons. She couldn't see one butterfly, couldn't make a single out of the swarm—so she wasn't really being caressed by one. She was being caressed. Universally. Totally. Everywhere. By all of them.

One hot, quick breath and they were many as one: the swarm reverse-fireworked into a huge hot mouth that kissed and sucked each of her medium-sized tits, pulling them in as if they were huge pink nipples. Sucking, pulling, twisting and squeezing—not damned mouths, but wringers and god-fuck-ing strong hands. Bruises, probably fuck-yes, but—Christ—she wanted to come! Then there came more lips inside those great suckers just for Cole's tight, aching nipples.

The come started somewhere in her cunt, somewhere that exploded up and through her like a wild pony ride of happy spasm. Her hips bucked and shook as her cunt sought something hard and thick inside her, or at least something fluttering and sweet on her throbbing clit—but the lips were single-minded and whoever was that single mind was sticking to just her nipples, her tits. Then they were a mass again, an orchestra of a billion tiny parts: tiny teeth nipping, pinching her tit-flesh, biting mouthfuls—

—she was being violated—

—out of her nipples till she screamed. The coming came without a mouth between her other lips, without a cock of meat or at least plastic in her cunt.

Tasting her own distant breath in the suit, Cole basked in twitching muscles and flickering eyelashes. It was the first time she'd ever come with someone (something) playing with just her tits. And, fuck was it good—

Blowing hard, heaving, she floated. Slowly, she opened one eye, seeing just for a flicker, a tiny butterfly perched on her nose, feverishly pulling at a cock no bigger than a bee's stinger.

For a flicker. Just. There was a jacking butterfly, then a rainbow-colored storm, then a hand that ran a Corinthian column finger down her belly.

It was a swirling inkpool of brilliance, vibrating, fluttering, larger-than-life, made of butterflies—and Cole wanted it in her pussy *now*. She wanted the whole goddamned thing, the swarm in her. She ached for, spread for—god, yes—butterflies.

—she was being taken—

One of her started the VRslang hand-gestures that would pop her chute and drop her back to the Liberty ship. The other of her started crying and just spread her legs wider. The hungry pussy won, and CANCELed. The gang-rape cock moved between her legs and spilled into her pussy, onto her clit. Not a fuck, a whale's head that really wanted to fuck her but then turned liquid and fluttering onto her clit's hard dot, pouring like heavy silver balls into her eager fuck-hole, and pressing towards her asshole. Eyes pressed phosphor-brilliantly shut, she could see with her pussy a hundred horny butterflies rubbing the globe of her clit, washing her basketball with their tongues, fucking its hot skin, stroking it like it was their own huge cock. A hundred thousand eager horny guys washing her great member with their hot tongues, stroking with their hard hands, milking her clit.

At her lips, down where she knew she was torrentially wet, she could feel the millions rubbing themselves on her lips, pulling, stroking, rubbing them as no mouth or finger of her size could. It was a fucking ballet dancing on the lips of her cunt.

Her asshole? Oh, they licked there, too—stroked there, and slowly pressed their many hungry hands and mouths inside.

There were butterflies in her, slowly, then eagerly, bucking against her G-spot and cervix. Her eyes flashed open, and she saw a pair of them on the end of her nose—and as the first ripples of a great deep-sea orgasm began in her wet, wet cunt, she watched one of them take his partner up the ass in a feverish, Eros-driven hard fuck.

Loved to watch, but Cole's eyes snapped shut in concentration on what was happening—lost herself in the tide of coming, in the breaking waves that snapped her jaws and arched her back. She was aware that she'd jetted, she'd ejaculated (and that very somewhere else, she knew that she'd have to wash her suit)—but that was the meat, the coming that came a second later rocked her, dazzled her, pushed her eyes open (butterfly sucking butterfly in a hummingbird 69), and she cried (yet again—gloriously again, religiously again) a deep bellowing scream that ebbed into exhausted near sobs.

Rolling down from the peak of the come, the fluttering mass became rolling waves of sensation. Caressed and fondled by a huge and gentle lover, a lover made of his own ocean waves, and flashes of pure color, she was THANKED in brilliant color for such a good fuck and then was wrapped in silk and furs and tucked into bed with a kiss on her cheek—

Hands stiff with clenching the bunk rails, Cole carefully pulled the facegear off, and creaked her head back into the cheap foam pillow. Every joint was aching—and her pussy throbbed, and her clit was sore with the suit's version of a butterfly fuck.

Javier, her bunkmate, wasn't there—so he missed Cole almost tearing her suit to shreds.

Maybe it was the still glowing memory of the butterfly fuck, or maybe it was the quick thought that she might have to sell the damned thing to afford to eat.

The Fabricscreen window on the side of her helmet, the little panel that showed her mileage for this trip—and her general bank balance—glowed with a row of angry red eggs that drilled into her shocked, then berserk eyes: BALANCE: 000.000.000.012.

She'd been *taken*, all right—

Smoke screen for a brilliant (well, fuck, she knew that) hack; a quick sneak under cover of a teeth-rattling come. She'd been violated, she'd *really* been taken—

Cole sat on her bunk, and couldn't help but think of the cost of butterflies: They certainly weren't free—

EVERYTHING BUT THE SMELL OF LILIES

She is wearing spandex pants decorated with the bold black and white icons of half a dozen Tokyo corporations. Her hair is in dreads, spiced with glittering watch parts. Her shoes are new and intelligent, contouring to her feet as she runs out of the crowd towards the place. Her poncho is tiger-striped, the newest Eurotrash fad, and the bystanders can see, as she pumps those strong legs in those black and white spandex pants, that she doesn't have a top on, and that her nipples (flashing out from under the red and black of the poncho) are only covered by crosses of black electrical tape. She is a mix of black and something else. All can see—even in the midnight glare of Broadway's brilliance of neon, lasers, fluorescents, and head-lights from blurring cars—that her skin is a brown like stained wood. Her face is high-cheekboned, her lips dark brown, her eyes hidden behind mirrored image-intensifying glasses.

She is running for her life: down the street, through the sidewalk crowd—panic in her strides and panting breaths.

It is drizzling, like static. The muscle at the door to the place don't like it because it messes up their radar goggles. The clients don't like it because it gets their furs and leathers all wet. The street drek don't like it cause it pisses off the money and the muscle and they usually take it out on who-ever is closest and can't afford to fight back. The limos come and go, a high-class and costly river of black plastic and steel. The rich's banter is light and sparkling above the rain and it blends, as only it could in the 21st century, with the chatter from the muscle's narrow-band radios.

She runs through the crowd, pushing streetdrek and citizens aside, glancing back over her shoulder at every opportunity. Panic lights her muscles, and she looks for someone to—

The words finally come out in an oscillating scream as she slams against the first ring of genetically-enhanced, neurochemically boosted, electronically hot-wired thugs. True to their purpose and few remaining authentic brain cells, they smash back—surrounding her with dense muscle and squealing radios and pushing her back into the crowd.

Her hands are grasping claws, her nails draw blood in a triad streak down the face of one of them (who didn't blink against his conditioning), and her legs hammer against his ballistic-nylon pants. Her scream sounds like some kind of a weapon and the few cheap, off-the-shelf guards pull their own and track the high windows around and up—unable to distinguish one crazed woman from an armed assault squad.

Then an arm snakes out of the crowd and with a clean, sure swipe slices her throat ear to ear.

The city is big, but not so big as to make the woman's throat opening up and a fine fanning spray of arterial blood commonplace. The muscle reacts first, being now freckled with potentially dangerous infected blood, and draws and aims...at nothing but the already twitchy street. At the sight of the weapons being quickly drawn and dropped to street level, anyone who has any kind of survival skills instantly turns and runs. To a streetful of people used to sudden urban violence, turning and running is called a riot. Luckily for the muscle and the few really innocent bystanders, the riot had a place to go: down the street like water down a cascade, away from the Men with Guns, away from the dangerous Blood, away from the Rich People being thrown into their cars by their over-reacting bodyguards.

The street is nearly quiet very soon after, save for the wailing of an approaching ambulance, called in a moment of rare altruism by one of the suits, and the last foaming, crackling bubbles from the woman's throat.

✹

The ambulance, one of the new Matzitas, arrives with a pulsing Doppler scream, parting the few bystanders who linger over the cooling corpse of the woman. Pulling up to the low curb, it clamshells open and coolly—as only micromechanicals and smartpolyplastics can—reaches out and touches her with the preciseness of Japanese manufacture. Like born, the medic steps from the uncoiling and undulating machines, orchestrating their movements with a palm-sized control unit.

Screened, probed, touched, sampled, sniffed, smelled, she is neatly picked off the cold and dirty sidewalk and swallowed into the ambulance's expanded interior.

Leaving behind the bodyguards giving statements to bored cops, the impatient suits, and the hungry stares of the onlookers, the ambulance closes with her and the medic inside and screams away.

✹

Death is too easy for me. See it every day. No, that's not the truth: Some days I sit in the hospital bay with the warm and humming ambulance and just wait for it. But the deaths I do see—the leaking, shrieking, whining, crying ones—reach beyond their occasions to swallow me, even when I do nothing but sit in the bay and watch teevee. One of those deaths can last days for me, stretching beyond its instant.

It's easy to die, when you're like me. I mean it's easy to die, period, man. Slip in the tub, get iced for your wallet, the new strains, acts of god—all of it man. Easy as pie to lie down and croak—and it's easy when you're like me to get right back up again.

I try not to get used to it, try not to have them stretch so far that they start to die in my dreams, when I eat, when I'm away from the ambulance. But I've been at it too long—they die in slippery, out-of-focus dreams and even when I sit down for dinner, soup becomes blood, meat becomes...meat. I look into everyone else's eyes and expect to see the things I've seen reflected back at me, but I don't. I don't know what they see, but it sure isn't what I see—what feels like every day.

Like me, yeah. Painful, sure, but you just gotta lie back and think of the money. Isn't that how it always is? Fucking for money, getting fucked for money—I just happen to get fucked over for money, that's all. The big fuck, maybe, but still...I'm a whore. A whore with a specialty, that's all. A real specialty.

I look at people differently, I guess. You do that when you see them dying, when you see them hurt and crying. I don't see them as they always look—smiling, laughing, getting angry...kissing or touching....I see them broken and leaking, discovering that they're meat and bones and blood. I see them in pain. Had a few girls in my life, even have two myself, now, but it's strange to see them, hear them and even crawl into bed with them when you see the things I see. I keep expecting them to break, to leak, to cry. I see it all the time—so often it doesn't seem right that they aren't hurting or dying.

Morley rigged it, the sick bastard. "There's a need, babe, a need we can fill." Yeah, you bastard—creeps like to fuck dead girls, so what do they need? You fucking guessed it. Problem is your usual dead chick will get all, kind of...unappealing after a point, right? What you need is a dead chick who can get up and walk out when the John's finished. What you need is me—or me after Morley.

Sometimes, the most real women I see are the ones who are lying still and cooling in the ambulance with me. The rest of them, the rest of the people I see, are just waiting to see me.

"Just rearrange you a bit," he says and gives me to his pals with the machines, the plastic parts, the implants. Technique noir, black tech, nasty bedroom tech. I remember one of them, this fat Chinese with skin like cheese—a clicking and whirring part of his face looking me over with god knows what: radar, microwaves, frigging sound for all I know. I remember him for the clicking and the whirring, and how he only spoke a few words of English. He also fucked me, I'm sure, while I was zoned under his machines, under his knife. My pussy smelled bad the next day, something that could've been come leaked out—smelled an awful lot like cheese, too.

Like this one, here: they look so peaceful, so rested and still. Their skin is so cool, so smooth. Even with the blood...but I can fix that, a little swipe with disinfectant, a dab or two with a biohazard absorbent towelette. Such a long wound, a thin slice from ear to ear. Clean, must have been a fractal knife, or a monomolecular wire. Still, she is beautiful. Striking. Frozen at the peak of her beauty by the knife, or maybe that wire. Her face is like a magnet, and I have a hard time doing the routine things I'm supposed to do. The implant and blood-screen fall away because of my entrancement. It's all I can do to sit in the back and let the ambulance drive itself to Mercy. She has high, sharp cheekbones; a nose with just enough of a upturn; lips full but not cartoonish. She has such a natural, wild look, this one has. I can see her not lying, cooling, chilling, in the back of my ambulance, her negative signs showing on half a dozen flatscreen monitors, but rather running under a hot sun somewhere, naked and warm, wild grasses shushing by her fine, perfectly turned legs, not-too-big, not-too-small breasts bobbing and swinging free and bare under the same glowing sun. She isn't a casualty, a DOA, a streetdrek; she is a primeval forest huntress, a priestess of a land long ago paved and sterilized.

I'm a corpse. I'm a professional victim, a stiff for hire. Pull my string (okay, slit my throat, strangle me), and I do my little number. And while I'm down there on your floor, on your bed, you can do whatever you want to do to me. Special job, as only Morley's dark doctors could have done. Don't know all of it myself—one lung gone for a refillable tank of air (so no breathing), blood now flowing through the back of my neck so my throat can get sliced or crushed if you like that kind of thing. On cue I get all cold, my nipples get all stiff, my cunt chills, my eyes lock up (in case you like to see your reflection in them when you fuck my stiff self) and I'm dead. Everything but the smell of lilies. Pay in advance, don't break the rules, and you can kill me, fuck me, and go back to the wife and kids. It's a living, dying is—

So beautiful. So natural she looks, even cooling and stiffening. She is a statue, an image on clear water. I try to be quiet, watching her, so as not to wake her. The image of her, quiet and still and not really, truly dead is so strong it's almost enough to dissipate the clean wound across her throat, the whining instruments all crying *she's dead* and the few specks of blood that remain on her poncho. Carefully, so as not to wake her, I move the poncho aside to better see her breasts—and so lovely they are: just the right size, somewhere between a nice cleavage and too small. They are fine, tight cones of deeply tanned skin. I can't see her nipples, covered as they are by crosses of tape (a recent style). I notice as I move the poncho that her pants end a bit below her navel, that her navel is pierced with a steel ring, and that she has the tiniest of bellies—a gentle rise to her stomach that seems so perfect on her. It adds something to her, this little belly does—when everyone can look like anyone (with enough money, of course) this little pot brings her right down to me, in the ambulance. She is a woman, a wild and fiery woman—all heat and hunger. Dead yes, but more alive than most of the meat I haul to the hospital.

Doesn't help that I like it. Yeah, Morley, make me into a dying doll. Yeah, you freaky creep, remake me so I can die on cue. Wouldn't work, you knew, if I didn't get off on it, too—maybe not croaking for every fat, rich slob, but—shit—I dig stepping into even the weirdest fuck's fucked-up trip. I don't get off, really, about lying here all dead, brain still clicking away but body faking being all cold and still, but I sure as shit do when I watch them hunp my stiff body. That's what gets me off, man, that's what Morley saw as he sucked my toes and came in my shoe—that I come when you come from doing your weirdest shit. I get off watching them all—yeah, Morely, too—dig down in their weirdest shit and make me do it. That fucking makes me come—

My still little angel. *Justine Moor, 27, type B+* the info from the ident card in her slim little wallet going past my eyes, into the mind of the ambulance. I watch her still chest, her fixed and dilated eyes. Even with a clotted line across her throat she is more alive that anyone I have ever seen. She is more alive, more vital, than Ruth or Vivian, than the other attendants at Mercy Hospital, than the doctors, than the people who flash by the window of the speeding ambulance. She is immobile, chilling but more alive than anyone, than me—I can't resist. She pulls me down to her with the force of her dead aliveness and I stroke the cool belly, run my quivering fingers up her sides to her lovely, pert breasts. I glide my hand up to cup them, to hold one like a still pillow, her nipples powerfully erect beneath the crosses of tape. My breathing is a hammer in my ears and my cock is painful iron in my uniform pants.

Yeah, Morley sure can pick them. "Justine," he said with that smile, that voice, "become a hardwired dead girl, a chilling and stiff-

ening hooker. A corpse for rent." Slice my throat, strangle me, fuck me—pay me. *Pegged me, looked right into these eyes and picked just the right job for a fucked up rent-a-corpse like me. Like tonight, man, Morley comes right up and says "—die for me, babe." Sure, no thought, no problem, man. I die for clients, right? So why shouldn't I die for my fucking pimp? Some bent job, some need for a diversion—what better than little me doing the poor streetdrek routine, right up to the suits and their rented guns, then Morley with his straight-edge right on cue to slice my pretty throat. Just another Saturday night for me. All I gotta do is get to the damned hospital, turn myself back on, get up and get out. Morley's got his distraction, I got my money. All is right with the—what the fuck? What's this guy doing? Shit, man, of all the fucking ambulances I gotta get one with a perv. Fucking-A, man, just my luck. Shit—*

So still and quiet. So perfectly frozen. Carefully, I remove the tape from her breasts. Her nipples are hard—little fingers, not thumbs. Deep brown like chocolate babies, wrinkled and hard like tire rubber. I taste one, the right one, and it reminds me of a pencil eraser dipped in chilled water. It seems to fill my mouth—the fear, the excitement, the humiliation making the universe balloon till there's just me, the background whine of the ambulance, and this dead girl's nipple in my mouth. My hand moves without me to cup the breast, to feel the weight of it, to gently squeeze to know its shape: it is a firm breast, a young breast. Not warm, no, but soft like silk with a thick African-mixed skin. Her skin has the weight of a black woman's but the color of coffee with way too much cream. As I lick and suck at her glorious nipple, my cock aches with the feverish pounding that fills my head and pushes the whine of the ambulance's electric motor to somewhere in the deep background. I hear the sound of my lips sucking and kissing her breasts and nipples. I hear my hammering heartbeat and the hurricane of my breaths going in and out.

What a fucking freak, man. What a professional, roaring, twister! The guys who do me know I can snap out and sit up, right? This guy ain't one. He's a corpse fucker and I'm his girlfriend, man. This guy ain't playing a fucking game with a specialty hooker. I almost switch my heart back on and take a nasty ol' breath and sit up and sock him one, right? But then I remember Morley, with his cold eyes and his jailhouse tattoo of chains going around his neck (one link per year) and I remember those chilling words: "Just give me enough time." And I'm fucked, I'm screwed, "cause it ain't been enough—not nearly enough—so I gotta lie down like the nice little stiff that I am. At least the guy knows how to suck a tit—dead or not.

I burst into flame, then. The heat of me blasts through my head and my cock and my lips. I kiss and lick her other nipple, squeeze and knead her other tit. She is cold under me, like from an ice water bath, but I am flaming, smoking from my lips and cock. Roughly, more rough than I would even have been with Ruth, Vivian—anyone breathing—I grab at her pants and give them a hard pull down, relishing in the smoothness of that glorious little belly. I get them down, and for the first time see her cunt. It is a glorious cunt, precisely shaved like hair was never there: a coffee-too-much-cream triangle padded with a delightful layer of so-soft skin. Her lips are tucked inside, so all I see is a faint brown crease, that delicious mons, and the hint of pearly clit. I struggle with her pants, stretching and pulling at the elastic stuff till I realize they are not coming off over her shoes. I quickly take out the safety shears and slice them away, leaving her strong legs and glorious cunt free. Now that I have completely fallen in, I am feverish and panicked: it is a long trip to Mercy, but not that long. I have minutes but not all that many. But, still, she is here, and my panic only adds an edge to my straining cock—

Fuck, fuck, fuck, fuck—not only a fucking corpse fucker but a fuck-

ing corpse rapist. *Shit, shit, shit! I almost pop my cork, blink and tell him to get the fuck away from my cunt when I remember again Morley's cold eyes and stay down. How many ambulances, man? How many tricks in this city? And I pick the two on the one night when I can't screw up. Great. Just. Great. Oh, man, not the fucking pants, man, they aren't cheap—oh, well. I'll get Morley to get me some others when I—oh, Jesus, this is one sick fuck, man, one sick fuck...*

I can't resist. Even dead her pussy is wine, a pure lovely vintage. In the cramped inside of the automatic ambulance, I get down between her strong legs and part them just enough—just enough to get my face down to her cunt, spread her lips and taste her. Her clit is big, her juices are chilled. Not white wine, red—not blood, just served cold, chilled. Her lips are so soft, like fine silk and I explore her cunt with my tongue, feeling her tiny inner lips, the hard cleft between her clit and her cunt proper. I slide my hand under her hard ass and squeeze, feeling the softness there, too, but also the relaxed, dead muscles that I could tell would have been iron, knotted steel when she was alive. Somewhere along the way I reach and grab my cock, start to roughly yank at myself, driven by the high-octane of her and the whine of the ambulance that I am sure, at any second, will drop as we enter Mercy's medical bays. My fear and disgust and excitement ram into me and makes my cock an iron, burning rod at my waist.

God, he's a fucking freak! My cunt's sopping, man. I'm dead and he's licking my corpse cunt, teasing my clit and I'm fucking coming. Can't move, can't until I pop my programming cork and climb all the way out of my "zombie" act, but that doesn't stop my clit from jangling like a bell. The comes echo and bounce around inside me. Can't cry, can't scream, can't grab the fucked-up freak's ears and jam his maniac face down hard onto my clit but, fuck, fuck, fuck I can damned sure fucking come. Can't scream, man, can't jerk and yell and cry and all that damned embarrassing stuff I do normally when someone's going after my clit like trying to dig the pearl out of an oyster, but I sure as fuck am coming and coming all over the place: I can feel it ripple and surge and tear and buck my brains out. My eyes are for crap anyway when I'm dead but now they're strobing and flashing all these gorgeous colors and all I can think, all the words that I can get to run through my head are that I hope he's so weird, so fucking bent, that he fucks me—cause I really want to get fucked, like, real fucking bad.

I want to fuck her. My cock hurts, and the one place, I know, that will make it feel so much better is the cold, wet and stiff confines of her cunt. With the taste of her still on my tongue and all over my face, I fuss and mutter with my belt and pants, finally getting them down as the ambulance rolls neat and computer-assisted into a high-banked turn and I know I have maybe five or ten minutes before the bay, before Mercy, to finish. My cock is finally out, and I clumsily position myself and move her cool legs out of my way. Despite the pain I feel from my cock, the horrible tension, I resist just sinking myself into her—wanting to make it last just so much longer until I taste her dead cunt with my cock—

Fuck me fuck me fuck me—fuck! I hate when they fucking tease! Get it in me you sick fuck, I scream in my paralysis, in my cooling and immobile jail cell of my reengineered and redesigned body. Fuck me, you sick fuck!

I sink myself into her. Her cunt is cool, but not cold—maybe my own heat warming her, maybe her core temperature is still pretty high. But you can't think of medicine and science when you fuck...fuck a corpse. I push myself in and feel her froth and juices swell around my cock, feel her tight yet loosening muscles surround and squeeze my cock. I think two things as I fuck her, my mind split by excitement and a cramping shame: I think of this beauty I am making love to, think of her incredible body, her nipple that I again put in my mouth and suck and kiss and nibble, and I think of fucking a sucking chest wound, of a sultry corpse, or a grave-rape. My cock is ramming, hammering into her beautiful cunt, into this delicious corpse and I tighten and spasm and jerk and scream as it all starts to come out—

Fuck fuck fuck—that's it, I've reached my top. How many fucking (fucking fucking fucking) times is a fucking corpse supposed to come, man? Fuck Morley and his rip, fuck him and me as his little distraction for the guards and the suits, I think the magic word, twitch that nerve-cluster I didn't have before Morley got his black medical hands on me, and I come up and out with a rush of heat, a screaming wave of fully reactivated nerves. I pull myself up and out of the grave, restart my heart, take a deep, painful, breath, feel my skin awake with an S/M crash of blasting pain (imagine your whole body falling asleep then waking up) and I scream into his face as he fucks me. I put my legs up and around and lock them behind his back, in that special place guys have just for this kind of thing and I fucking ride his own screaming bucks. He lets go of my nipple and gives me the cutest look of pure lust and fear I have ever seen, but the sick fuck doesn't stop fucking, doesn't stop jerking himself into and out of my now-warming, now steaming honey-pot. He screams and yells and keeps fucking then jerks and squirms—

I ain't done yet, man, I ain't at all done yet. I push and pull on his stiffening and quivering muscles until I've had my own—and it comes like it has never come before: a fucking torrent of good stuff crashing down and all over me and I scream like I never screamed for Morley, for a client (when they're into murder), I scream the best scream I have ever screamed, bucking and clawing at his cooling back until I can't move any more—

✳

The ambulance arrives at Mercy. It whines, fading to a simple warning burst of sound as the medicals pour from the hospital's service bays. Nestling into its sockets and data-ports, it opens organic and precise, spilling out its gurney into their waiting arms.

With technological precision, the body is brought into an emergency suite and the hospital sets to work with a array of micro-surgical tools resembling a squirming, undulating, chrome palm frond. Fluids are pumped, charges are sent, nanomachines are injected, and even a cloned and altered heart the size of a large orange is mated to his body. These and many other (as many as his body and minimal medical insurance can stand) attempts are made but in the end, after some four or so minutes, his body is simply dumped into the hospital's vast and frightening organ storage facilities for recycling—and his next-of-kin is automatically sent an apologetic videomail message.

✳

Walking home through a drizzle that is creeping towards a hard rain, she doesn't feel any of it. Some stare at the pale gash that runs from under one ear and across her throat to end at her other ear—but since it closely resembles a new young fashion statement, most dismiss it casually.

Justine doesn't think all that much as she walks the three miles back to her capsule apartment, but once she thinks very, very clearly, cleanly: *Morley, Morley, Morley...I hope it was a good score, a grand score. You owe me, you motherfucker and you owe me big—*

You sure can pick them, Morley: next time I get to fuck a corpse— next fucking time, man, you get to be all cold and stiff.

Hope you like playing the corpse, man. Cause I just developed a new—hmm—taste...

FULLY ACCESSORIZED, BABY

Lower Shanghai, the dark and deep port section, pulsing slow and steady with a red, black, red, black, red, black rhythm of cheap neon and fractured laser light. Inside, up there in that flat, it was a silent optical backbeat for the two of them.

One of them sat on a black futon couch, watching, just watching. Her ID called her Ms. Hakata, and the register kept the illusion going. Val wasn't told what to call her, and so stood there in front of her and the blackness of the futon, in the red, black, red, black neon pulse and didn't move.

"Get rid of that," Cox said, waving a glowing THC stick tip in Val's direction.

THWAP, plastic raincoat flopped on the floor. The tension avoided artistic metaphors of dull cocoons. Val stood in front of her client, in front of an obviously unfriendly Cox, in a simple black number: black cotton dress, short enough to show smooth knees, good calves; sleeves short enough for creamy upper arms; neckline low enough to show that they were really that big.

"And that—"

—they really were. The simple black landed on the tami with the same cool drop, and Val stood there in lingerie glory: black lace push-up pushing up same creamy as those upper arms. 38-somethings, probably upper scale, and the one thing you don't bring with you to a high-class playroom in the dark shadows of Shanghai is a tape measure. Upper 30s. Just as Cox had ordered. When you have the yen, you get what you want.

And a single opera-length latex glove.

Silk panties, basic but fem enough for that little pad of tissue to show. Garter belt. Very fem, but on those hips it worked. Riding low and tight (but not cutting, no wire through cheese), but the legs were the very best. Fine as something that had walked out of some museum. The hose were silk and fine, but were nothing but shade and shadows on those perfect pins.

Cox was a leg lady. Picked it up somewhere, and enjoyed it too fucking much. The tits, she'd typed into the datanet, to the Theatre, had to be upper 30s-something, but the legs, ah, those legs had to be *fine*.

Yeah, you get your yen's worth. And she had spent enough on this: Money worth it.

"And that—"

The name of the game and everyone knows it from the Theatre and its huge client base and talent scouts to little Val here and the hotel manager to everyone who knows the business is to *Get the Client Off*—

The bra dropped and Val's tits didn't. Ah, but they didn't hang there like some kind of silicone joke, they sagged just enough for Cox's trained gaze to figure a good job, at least. Ah, but pretty, pretty, pretty. Cox was in a simple black kimono— simple in its expensive silk and basic style. Nothing to get in her way as she spread her own legs just enough to not appear too hungry (this is about control, and even if the game was to Get the Client Off it doesn't do to have it happen while the property smiles at your own dripping cunt/mouth) and ran a finger from cunt mouth to clit and stopped and pressed—

"And that thing—"

Shaved. Val was heavy in a sex kitten kind of way—just enough for smooth curves and gentle slopes. Not fat, not that far, but not the bones and ligaments that Cox had twisted in her own body from running, dealing, scoring and heavy celebrations. Val's was a milk-fed body, a pampered machine engineered and scalpeled to hit the requirements of a culture and a type: hard fine legs, baby-smooth yet taut stomach, tits that lifted high and fine and big enough to play with and hard enough to play with but not things that would fall into her armpits when you finally got her down on the bed.

"Okay," Cox said, "—now that—" waving towards the single right glove.

It came sloooowwwwly off—inchworm of hot, sticky latex, the one piece of the outfit that definitely didn't belong—and so had to come off. Inchworm, inchworm of soft, pale skin....

Cox watched the de-gloving with glued attention, eyes never leaving the act, the arm. As she sat, engrossed, one of her own harder, callused, hands dropped down to her crotch. Kneading, she watched. Working her own hand in, and onto her clit, she watched the glove.

Pale flesh, then the pink plastic gasket ring of a Mitsubishi implant. High-quality. Wet-pussy, state-of-the-art: no Korean polymers, no French stainless. Cox asked for, and got, a fuckin' Mitsubishi.

The hand was a fine-tooled example of the marriage in harmony of the best in Japanese prostheses and aesthetics. It was fine teak, polished smoother than the hand it had replaced, set with matte-black joints and cables with undulating polymer cords. Cox could tell that it was telling Val all a real hand would have—the freckles of sensory nipples and the compound microfibers that ran through the teak like veins were a sign of someone who hadn't just sold her right arm for an arm. Val had sold her right arm for something far better.

Insert slightly embarrassing moment here; as Cox flexed her long, hard body up to get a twist of the kimono out of the crack of her ass. Bottomless, she spread her columnar legs and made a quick, flighty gesture with her own mere flesh and mere blood right hand "—Put over there—"

Val smiled a geisha smile, as cool as the hand she latexed

with a surgical glove, as cool as the quick squirt of Adventure-lube™ she spurted into the gloved Japanesque hand—

The little girl knelt down in front of the big girl, an act that could never be called embarrassing or clumsy. It was part of the strip, part of the act, part of fucking. It was a never-touch foreplay that started with Val standing on her heels and looking down, geisha cold, at Cox and sinuously gliding down to a hot squat before the rocky Cox.

With her cold hand, she parted Cox's shaved lips. Cox moved a bit here, to comfort herself, to ease her worker's body into the birthing, fist-fucking, position. She spread open wide, and watched the frozen smile of Val as she eased one, then two, then three into her warm, hot, hotter, fucking, steaming, cunt.

Inside, back and forth. Inside, hot and foaming with cunt juice. This is what the customer wanted, this is what the customer ordered. Her cunt was used to this, and with a twist, and a swing wide of strong worker legs, Cox...just...simply...opened up. Give Val credit, she knew that hand, that Japanese tech prosthesis, she knew the insides of a woman, knew the architecture. She drove the warm, carved wood into Cox's cunt.

Inside, gloved by the customer's cunt. Val sat there for a while, watching Cox's face as Val eased the pointed fingers into thump-grabbed fist. It was a precise working of precise machinery into the cunt, and Val did it with the taste of a microsurgeon, the breath of a midwife. Gradually, Cox moved herself onto the hand, that fine fucking machine, she started to ride and churn her pussy around the hand. Val knew the fuck, knew this was the love of this kind of fist-fuck, this was the love of it, this was the glory of it, this was getting to fuck that glorious Porsche or BMW. This was getting behind the wheel of a glorious piece of engineering and riding the gearshift till orgasm rounded the fucking bend.

The deep come, the cunt come was hard and pressed. It squeezed down on the Mitsubishi prosthesis like a hot handshake. It was a quickie, true. It was sudden, true. But it was only the first dip in the tango.

Slowly, Val let Cox push the Mitsubishi out. Easy, designed that way, a fist engineered for fisting: a fist made with the smooth precision of a Swiss—*excuse*—Japanese watch, and it collapsed down into almost nothing at all with the same single-mindedness of design.

A breather in the action: Val removed the glove from her hand. Cox took a sip of water from a black plastic tumbler. Val stood at rest. Cox moved next to the sofa, to a small black nylon bag.

"You're what I asked for, right?" Cox.

"Yes, Sir." Val.

"You've got all I asked for, right?"

"Yes, Sir."

"Take it out then."

She did. Bigger than maybe the panties could have hidden. Maybe some kind of new special effect that inflated from something so small as to make a perfectly bulgeless panty. Looked meaty enough though, long enough but not so as to look like a prop, or a bad leatherman fantasy. Not Tom of Finland, but Val of Shanghai. It was a good seven inches of curving dick. All Cox asked for; long enough to use, without being a waste.

"Play with it. Make it hard."

The point of it, really. The Mitsubishi. After a quick bow and grab at a tube of lube, the turned wood and fine electronics started to work it, pulling it like taffy to start, but as blood did what blood will do, it went from torpid to engorged and then ramrod fucking hard in the streetlight glare from beyond the windows.

"Good girl," Cox said, playing with her pussy in a lazy, distracted kind of way.

The cock was stretching and reaching up—bending in that

special way that good cocks do when they get very hard. In the flashing red, black, red, black, red, black of Shanghai, little Val with the big pretty tits got her cock all hard and gleaming in the flicker.

"Work it good, now. Work it good—" Cox said.

—and Val did just that. Did it with a spit of lube and an off-the-shelf right hand. Her cock was a gleaming pole in that flicker, all for the joy of Cox, all for the hungry eyes of Cox. Those eyes and that same gleaming pussy, her legs spread wide and inviting. The customer stroked her cock and watched the hungry cunt of Cox, watched as she rubbed the little nib of her clit, and Cox watched Val stroke her cock.

"Good. And. Hard—" Cox said in a breathy, husky voice, and Val, who had the genes for the cock, but not for those tits, knew from a long time of being with those tits and others in these (similar) situations, knew that a come had come and Cox's eyes had dimmed in that inward pulse—

"—not you," Cox said, just as Val was going to. But Val was a good girl (she was), and instantly stopped stroking her cock. It wasn't easy to stop. Dead. Still. But she was a good customer, a good girl and she did. There (please, hope, please, hope) was something better, even better, coming next.

Cox was digging and churning up her bag, looking for something, Val saw, amid modules, boards, clips, insulated canisters with the yellow eye of BIOHAZARD BIOTECH SPECIMENS, until—"Ah!"—she came out with a cock maybe just a wee bit smaller than Val's.

"Show me where you want it," Cox said to the customer.

Ah, what a choice, what a decision: to wrap tongue, or spread cheeks? Not much of a choice really—even though Val was drooling with the Need to Come, it was her asshole that really wanted this piece of cybernetic cock. Wanted it in deep and hard and fast—damnit now!

Her mouth was watering, and if it could, so would her asshole. The cork was out and the words, at the thought of that state-of-the-art cock in her aching asshole: "Come on, I want it! Come on, come, ON! Please, Mistress, Mommy, please I want it bad, I want it deep, I want it hard, I want to taste it all the way through me. Please, please, please! Mommy, God, I need it so bad, right fucking now—"

Cox was deep in the ritual of the preparation to fuck. Off came the bunched and binding kimono, out came the tube of Neurolube™ and with it was bathed the cock, the fucking bit of tech, the silicone—all warm and soft and just fucking right for fucking—in the lube. It was a perfect piece for this perfect piece: it was a beauty of sculpted penis-ness. Not a cock, not a penis, no, no, no, it was a woman's dick, an asshole's dick. It was fine and turned and formed just to be a fucking machine. One end was the gripper, the rings of the internals of it, the faint glimmer of surgical sensors and motor grippers, and the hilt that separated it from the sculptured cock. Between the gripping root and the lovely shaft and head, the ring was covered with even more sensors and motors and a flicker, and all that just right stuff that would fit (and did!) so perfectly with plastic neatness around Cox's hot, fucking hot, clit.

The gripper went in, the sensors and flickers fitted right over her throbbing little penis, and Cox was ready to fuck.

—as was little Val, just what she'd asked for. Just what she'd ordered, just what she needed.

Snapping on a glove, Cox moved behind the panting Val. Kneeling, Cox gripped those nice hips, circled Val's little fuckhole with a shiny finger, drawing, and testing, and touching till her asshole just reached up and grabbed her finger, and sucked at it like a hungry mouth.

"Fucking ready—" Cox said, as Val said the same.

Val moved back arching, trying to swallow Cox's cock. "Hungry bitch—" Cox said, almost pulling back with a nice bite of Top, of Bitch, of Cunt, of all-around meanness, but the cock felt too good inside Cox and the buzzers and stimulators and hummers and flickers against her clit and the neurofibulator inside her aching cunt was just too good for her and for her role. She fucked and kept on fucking, slapping her strong thighs against Val's so soft thighs, slapping and slucking (no other word) the music of a good hefty ass fuck, a fuck of an asshole so ready and eager and swallowingly hungry.

Val arched and screamed and bucked and pushed against the pushing and moaning Cox. Covertly, because she really needed to and because she wanted to come now more than anything in the whole damned planet, Val was yanking her own cock. She was twisting and pulling; starting to feel the come make its hard way up through her dick and through her asshole into her mouth—

And found an echo in Cox. Yeah, it was nothing anyone would believe, but, fuck, as they both would say after for some time, it was what had to happen, what really did happen—and Val's legs gave out and she grunted to the floor on top of her aching cock (feeling so good she didn't notice the pain from the other drugs of happiness in her system), the weight of Cox on top of her—also aching, also twitching the hi-tech dick out of her aching asshole and onto the bunched and torn tami mats.

Vibrating, humming, pause.

They got up, kissed and more kissed, smiled and more smiled, and got dressed, touching and kissing as they did, knowing that this wasn't the last time, that all they had to do was dial in, and clickity-clack on a terminal.

They were done, done, done, and done, too. When and if they compared notes (maybe) they'd realize (maybe) that they'd both paid, they'd both been submissive client to the dominant client. They'd been done, all right—

But then they were also fully cooked and smiling.

If it was really good, who cared who paid?

THE NEW MOTOR

It is not our place to say, via hindsight, what exactly happened that one particular night. It's easy to dismiss, with scorn or even a kind of parental, historical fondness, to say that he was just visited by vivid dreams, a hallucinatory fever, a form of 1854 delusion (after all, we smile, frown, grimace, laugh or otherwise, this was 1854), or some hybrid kin of them all: A vision one third unresolved traumas, one third bad meal of steak and potatoes, one third 19th-century crippling social situation. What we cannot dismiss—because it's there with minuscule precision, in detailed blocks of blurry type in rag pulp sidebills, in the fine-filigreed pages of the genteel or just the skilled—is that John Murray Spear, a spiritualist of some quite personal renown and respect, did indeed depart Miss August's Rooming House for Gentlemen of Stature (near the corner of Sycamore and Spruce in Baltimore, Maryland), and go forth to tell anyone who would listen—and some did, as those newspapers reported and those diaries told—about his visitation by the Association of Electricizers.

Close your eyes, metaphorically, and envision the images that might have fluttered through the expansive and trained consciousness of Mr. Spear as he lay barely waking on a cheap mattress more tick than stuffing, the too-warm embrace of a humid Baltimore summer morning pouring through the thin gauze of the window. Amid the jumble and clutter of a day's thoughts, they walk—as contemporary A. J. Davis expressed it: "spirits with a mechanical turn of mind"—into the far-reaching mind of John Murray Spear.

Perhaps gears lit with fairy energies, they turn and tumble through his waking, shining metal honed with eldritch tools, playing inadvertent peg-toss with his sheet-raising morning priapism. Maybe a great churning clockwork contraption whose complexity echoes Medusa's curse of knowing equally insanity or death. Or they might have taken the form of a Con-Ed employee in bedazzling ethereal refinements, in a saintly pose of divine grace while the animated logos and mascots of every power company that was, is, and will be flitted around his nuclear halo—commercial cherubs to His crackling, humming, arcing power.

Their form was something that even escaped Spear himself, for when he spoke of their visitation—and he did, oh yes, he did from his own mount and other less spiritual soapboxes—a 220-watt gaze seemed to consume him and his articulations became less detail and more impact. "Their form," he said to his breakfast companions and often, for many weeks thereafter to any stranger on the street, "is fast and incorporeal. I don't possess the mind to express their appearance in words, but their message, dear—" Sir, Madam, Officer, Friend "—is clear and ringing in my ears: Go forth, they spoke, go forth and with these two simple hands bring into the world a machine, a great work of engineering, that would take motive power from the magnetic store of nature, and therefore be as independent of artificial sources of energy as this, our own human body. Go, this conglomeration of spirits pronounced, and build the Physical Savior of the Race, The New Messiah...the New Motor!"

John Murray Spear did, indeed, say these words from that reasonably expensive boarding house in summer heated Baltimore, to the swampy humidity of the capital, then upward toward the cooler environs of the Northeastern states. He spoke of the visitation of the Electricizers to a shocked and tutting crowd of theosophists in Providence, his hypnotic description of the coming glory of the Motor and how it would bring about a new Age of Man Through Machine ticking out of sync with their slowly shaking, disbelieving heads.

He spoke of the Motor in Boston before a hall not as packed as it had previously been for the spiritualist of some repute, and answered with complete sincerity questions of the Motor's construction ("things of this earthly sphere coupled with the energies of transcendent motion and ethereal force..."), creation ("for a small donation you can speed its manifestation and arrival here, to us..."), method of operation ("Can one envision a locomotive, some new machine of human use and creation, that might come during the new millennium? The works of the Motor may be visible to some of us with the enriched spiritual vision, but the true powers of it will be as unseen as that machine of ages undreamed..."), and patentability ("if the material servants of this, our Government of Country, should grant me the license of its manufacture then I see no reason not to accept...").

Coal and snow beard, hair wild with his feverish retellings, supple (for a man of his forty summers) body bending wildly with each description of the glory of the Motor and Spear's saving of mankind through its mechanical enlightenment, Spear made himself a sight as he traveled. For some, he was a sight that brought smiles, frowns, or sadness at his state of affairs. But as he slowly, town by town, street by street, meeting by meeting told his tale, made his claims, his entreaties, he gathered people who listened earnestly to his description of the Mechanical Savior of the Race, the New Motor.

With each meeting they watched, drawn by him and his description of the action of the Motor. Again, we can only imagine what they saw in the older, yet virile and definitely passionate Spear. Men enticed by the engineering spirituality—this was, after all, 1854, a time when all of the world's ills seemed to have the potential of being cured by the right use

of the steam engine—their members enlivened by the churning, throbbing, mechanizations of the Motor; women
enraptured by the...*hard* drive of Spear himself, and the
license to become excited by something—assuredly, what
could be safer than something not obviously sexual such as
the New Motor? So, with male members erect and throbbing
at the thought of the Mechanical Savior of the Race, the New
Messiah, and female sexes flowering and moist, equally, at the
thought of driving pistons, churning cams, humming fly-
wheels, twirling governors, rasping bellows, and other,
pounding, sliding, gleaming parts (some the Motor's, some
Mr. Spear's) they went from couple to few, smattering to intimate gathering, dinner party to small crowd—with John
Murray Spear and his clockwork choir invisible at the intangible controls.

Trickling together, their small number slowly gathering
into a very small belief, they worked their way to the High
Rock of their faith: A small farmhouse just outside of Lynn,
Massachusetts. As to why they stopped...guesses include that
the small hamlet of saltbox houses and cod fishermen was a
perfect harmonious position from which to assemble the various physical attributes that would form the birth stage of
their divine appliance, that the small religion had found a
home in the craggy, intolerant faces of the townspeople, or
that, simply, they had run out of cash.

For reasons ultimately unknown, Spear and his traveling
companions stopped, took a collective breath and, perhaps
checking their wallets, purses and secret stashes, determined
that the soil, the homes, the people, the weather there would
be ideal, and—at the direction of their engineering apostle—
set out to assemble the reason (perhaps) for their
companionship. There, they set out to actually create the
Mechanical Messiah, Clockwork Jesus, Divine Device, Holy
Contraption, their New Motor.

Looking more and more the father of a screaming-in-infancy religion and less the mad seer, Spear dispatched his believers and, along with them, like hosts of the realm, the few remaining coins in their possession. "Cyrus, you shall go and fetch wheels of varying sizes. Be certain that their weight not be so great as to preclude their turning with ease," Spear said to the young engineering student whose face, marred by smallpox, was hidden by a great black beard. "Your task, Youngfellow, is to purchase wire with the correct vibrations. I trust you, above anyone else, to recognize these vibrations by the wire's feel between the fingers," Spear said to the old railway man who shook with a consumptive cough when excited, which was often. "Bartholomew, you shall acquire cylinders of rosy copper," Spear told the rather too pretty, and too dandied, young lad from New York. "I need your fine eye, Mary, to go and bring us only canvas of good quality, as for the making of bellows," Spear said to the old matron whose single eye was a disturbing too-blue. "Eunice, you go and seek out strips of tanned hide so that belts may be employed in the creation of the divine Motor," Spear said to the stone-stern, and perpetually unsmiling, headmistress.

And so each was sent, little money and elaborate instructions in hand, out into the town of Lynn—till Spear remained with but one of his machine-enraptured flock.

"Faith, you of the beautiful gaze, the arresting demeanor, you shall remain with me while the others acquire the necessary physical requirements of our Mechanical Savior, for I am in need of your...*assistance* to prepare what shall become our High Rock, the seat of the birth of our Mechanical Deliverance into Glory!" Spear said to the handsome maiden with hair the color of hot embers, eyes that danced with a sparkling entreaty to be gazed into, a bosom full and firm, and so-shapely, so-perfectly formed ankles (oh, momma!).

✵

"What a wonder this day we create, Faith: something with the aspects of the earthly, mated with the spiritual. This will be a true marriage of elemental forces," John Murray Spear said, with breathy passion, eyes dancing with fierce intensity.

"Tell me more, Mr. Spear. Oh, please, enlighten me on our great mission. Speak of it more!" Faith said, stepping close—very close—her eyes also lit with passion...though of a more earthy nature.

"Ours will be a creation that will align the chaotic nature of this sphere, a mechanical messiah that will deliver us from our primitivism on this plane," Spear said, stepping equally close, his hands seizing her sleeves—his heat conducting even through the thick, scratchy material.

"Oh, yes, Mr. Spear...John...speak of this Motor we build," Faith said, pushing her body hard against his.

"Ours are but the hands...Faith...nothing but the physical extensions of the Association of Electricizers, those who have blessed us with the information to see to its noble creation," Spear said, his hands dropping, grazing the slope of her protected chest.

"Yes...our 'physical extensions.' I know what you mean, John. I am so proud to be their...your...hands in this," Faith said, taking his hands in hers and placing them on her heaving bosom.

"The Motor is their will, with our physicality, towards a mutually beneficial union where we shall both be able to achieve new heights of enlightenment," Spear said, his hands working the delightful fullness of her breasts.

"Oh, yes, John, speak to me of our impending...enlightenment," Faith said, hastily unbuttoning the front of her blouse, fingers dancing a frenzy.

"We cannot know of the full impact of the Motor on our essences—can the ant know the dreams of men? When the Motor is infused with the pure force of life, we shall be brought up to unparalleled heights," Spear said, helping her shuck off her blouse, and then part her pale underthings.

"Oh...*John*...what a wonder the Motor shall be!" Faith said, bringing her hands forward to squeeze and caress her breasts, relishing in the sensual ache.

"It will indeed be one, Faith—a true miracle. And we shall be here to see its creation and then its...birth," Spear said, his hands echoing her own—then, lowering himself to the dirty floor of the farmhouse, gently he took one of her breasts (the left) in his hands and kissed the swollen pink nipple.

"...Oh, Lord, John...oh, Lord...yes, such miracles...," Faith said, sighing with deep passion—a rich, throaty sound as Spear kissed, then licked, then sucked at her tight nipple.

"Yes, Faith—we are truly fortunate to be here at this time, to be involved with this momentous delivery...," he said, lifting the billows of her skirts, pushing aside the linen curtains.

"...Oh, yes, John...so *fortunate*...," she said as he rustled undergarments, hands fluttering against her quivering thighs.

"We are blessed, Faith, so...blessed...," Spear said ferociously moving cotton until a triangle of silken red hair was revealed. This, too, he kissed—at first with gentle contacts, and then with more and more penetrating intensity.

"...," Faith said, which translated as a breathy moan accompanying a reflexive push downward with her sex to get more of his tongue into her.

"...," Spear said, which translated (same language) as fumbling his too-stiff, throbbing penis free of many similar layers of itchy clothing. When his bare hand met same of his member, a sigh only momentarily interrupted his work on her well-lubricated region.

This went on, mutually pleasurable to both parties, until an ecstatically explosive orgasm vented up through her, spilling into his mouth as a gush of slightly salty fluid.

Almost spent himself, he rocked back onto his haunches and then onto the floor of the farmhouse—his shockingly hard organ pointing authoritatively straight up, tipped by a pearlescent drop of fluid.

"We are witnesses to the creation, and the birth, of a divine engine—" Spear said, pushing himself up, struggling to embed himself in the slippery, hot recess of her molten sex.

"We are...helping the mechanical forces of the...*oh, God!*" she said, seeing his need, excited by his need, and lowering herself carefully to straddle, then feed his male member into her too-hot, too-silken, too-wet entrance. Feeling the fat tip of him push, then slide up into her, a musical moan of delight escaped her bitten lips.

"We are the orchestrations of the creation of an engineering messiah—*oh, oh, oh!*" he said as she eased herself down, stuffing herself with his erect manhood. Then, with escalating intensity—driven by a need as old as humanity itself—she began a repetitive rhythm: up and down, up and down, up and down—a liquid, slapping motion that ebbed with his member almost escaping the lips of her sex, and peaked with him filling her to her utmost capacity.

After an uncertain time, their moans and cries and incoherent bursts of near-speech, near philosophical-balderdash, synched perfectly then climbed, a pair of syncopated screams, toward a deity that they hoped to perhaps outdo with their engineered divinity, their mechanical savior.

Passion echoing down into an exhaustion that began to firmly pull them down into sleep, Faith and John Murray Spear managed to extricate themselves from their primitive embrace of genitals, adjust their voluminous and very often scratchy clothing, and put on somewhat civil faces for the rest of their congregation as they returned from their errands.

✳

...An 1854 contraption, but surreally hinting at the complex
technologies of our current civilization: A personal computer
made of glass mason jars, coils of copper tubing, sheets of tin,
old wagon wheels and the remains of a pot-bellied stove
(Apple logo painted on one corner, optional).

...A machine of a previous century, a maddeningly complex clock—an interdimensional mandala of impossibly
interlocking gears, fantastically meshing wheels, magically
transversing pendulums, and springs coiling into eye-smart-
ing spirals.

...A 19th-century Rube Goldberg contraption of perilous
articulations: the egg rolls down the tin gutter, lands in the
funnel, which trips a lever that drains water from a jug and
fills a bucket, lifting a cork, relaxing a string, tightening a
bow, firing the arrow, hitting the target, ringing the bell—and
on, and on, into a cascading eternity.

... An age-of-steam cyclotron: a tremendous squeezing
weight pressing down through the action of great screws and
pulleys onto a complex box of tightly spinning gears that,
action reproduced on an molecular level, tried to split atoms
like a hammer with an anvil.

The New Motor, the Divine Device, the Mechanical Savior
of the Race could have looked like any of those—but rather,
embarrassingly, it just sat there: a cold collection of parts taking up a major part of the farmhouse.

"Arise, spirit of the Machine! Awaken, Spiritual Engine! Be
given the force of Life, O Magnificent Instrument—breathe,
beat, tick, hum, click, whir (come on, damnit!)," intoned (then
whispered) John Murray Spear standing before the inert pile
of metal, and other, parts.

"Hear my words, New Motor—hear then and take of our
essence, borrow of our life to spark your action! We are here,
Great Ethereal Mechanism, and we exist so that you may oper-
ate and live!" Spear said, passion building, then smashing

through his words—ringing them off the farmhouse walls and slowly reaching (especially one of) his congregation.

"It is time, Motor, time for your automated birth so that you might lead us into a New Age!" John Murray Spear said, words ringing out, echoing with noble desire—and sparking a more human version in one particular person.

"Now, Motor—*Now!* My voice, my spiritual essence reaches out to you, oh, Holy Implement of the Association of Electricizers, and sparks in you the motive power, the magnetic store of nature!" Spear thundered, the energy of his passion stirring (yes, one more than the others) those present to feel their own thrilling charge of excitement.

So spoke Spear, intonation after intonation, plea after plea, summons after summons till his flock panted, eyes glazed and hearts pounding, themselves reeling from the charge he was raising—even if the New Motor, dead as anything, still sat immobile.

One of them, even more charged, heart more pounding, eyes even more glazed, was so seized by the driving determination, the impassioned oration of Spear, by a physical manifestation of his determination...her legs failed her and she fell to the floor and her hands, moving like enchanted serpents, plunged beneath her skirts and began to feverishly work her melting sex in ecstatic syncopation.

Also feeling the charge of Spear's oration, the rest of the little New Motor flock was similarly energized, though not, definitely not enough to get down on the rough floor and begin to masturbate. Still, to be fair, they didn't stop her from continuing either—

Complex skirts pushed up and out of the way, she spread her pale thighs wide so as best to gain access to her aching sex—her pulsing, liquid, burning nether regions that so desperately ached for contact, stroking, rubbing, penetrating release.

Hands a fluttering sensual dance at her swollen lips, quivering vulva, and pulsing clitoris, she worked and worked and worked some more until a shattering orgasm applauded Spear's spiritual conjuration of the New Motor—

—and then, slowly, achingly, but also *definitely*, it started to click, then to whir, then to vibrate, hum, oscillate, revolve, and otherwise simply *move*...the Physical Savior of the Race, the New Messiah, the New Motor began to work.

And Faith, exhausted, smiled, smiled, smiled—

✱

Sometime later, the flock—in their less-than-comfortable cheap beds, but too tired with celebration to mind—became lost in dreams of glorious spiritual engines. Spear stood before the great (pick one description, but now filled with motive life) machine, eyes still wide after many hours.

"So...incredible. In my dreams...no, not even in my most vivid of dreams could I ever have imagined the beauty of you, Motor. No, I could never have envisioned the glory of your movement, the power of your functioning. I am enraptured with your mechanism—"

"John," Faith said—also tired, but not quite tired enough for bed—touching her priceless spiritualist on the shoulder. "Please, John, can I, may I...again?"

"You are truly the Mechanical Messiah, Motor. You are the Divine Engine. I am your servant and engineer—humbled before your actions, your motions—" Spear said, eyes only for the vibrant contrivance.

"John, my body—I need you, John. You have awakened me, John. I need to feel you again," Faith said, voice heavy with desire, clutching firmly Spear's arm.

"Nothing, Motor—nothing on this earth shall keep me from my service of your gears, your parts, your elements. I shall be your Priest of the Oil Can, your Deacon of the Wrench, your Bishop of Repair.... I am yours, Motor, and no one else's," Spear said, glazed sight enraptured with awe at its motions.

"Please, John, I want you. I need you—please don't make me beg, John. Please—" Faith said, tears gleaming on her cheeks, tugs becoming more insistent.

"Great Implement of the Association of Electricizers, your motion grants me the greatest joy! I am here—I am here for you now, Messiah. My life as of today is yours. Your nuts I will tighten, your belts I will lubricate, your spokes I will straighten, your glass I will polish, your metal I will make gleam with my dedicated hands and all the strength granted me in this fleshly shell—" Spear said, pulling away from the woman and stepping closer, bathing in the technological glimmer of his holy gizmo.

"John, you cocksucker, are you going to fuck me or not?" Faith said, or words of an 1854 equivalent said, screaming into his ear over the dim of the machine and the single-mindedness of his locked gaze.

But to her own impassioned, driven, passionate pleas and invocations all John Murray Spear said was, "—what was that again, Motor? What is it you need? What is it my Physical Savior of the Race, my New Messiah? What do you require of myself, your most humble servant? The tightening of some wayward screw, the adjustment of some loose belt, perhaps. I am yours, Motor—tell me what you desire and I shall sate it!"

Faith said something else at that point, but since even the 21st-century version would have scorched a sailor's ears we won't reproduce it—suffice it to say that whatever it was that she...*screamed,* Spear wasn't listening.

So Faith left John Murray Spear, left him standing bathed in the electric glow of the New Motor, the Divine Device, his Clockwork Jesus, and went out and down the road, consumed with frustration and a self-righteous fury, into the small hamlet of saltbox houses and cod fishermen, to tell them a very interesting tale.

✳

We might not know if John Murray Spear actually had his vision of the Association of Electricizers; don't have a clue as to what his creation, the New Motor, even looked like. We haven't the foggiest idea of how it became active, or that it even did—all this is lost to hazy history, fragmented memories; not even reported in the documents we do possess. But we do know some things. We know, for instance, as stated of Spear's gathering of his flock of his speaking to the residents of the eastern seaboard; that the Mechanical Messiah, the Holy Contraption, the New Motor was built in Lynn, Massachusetts and that it was destroyed shortly after its activation by the outraged Christian citizenry of that small hamlet of saltbox houses and cod fishermen.

But the truth really doesn't have anything to do with this story. All facts do is pin the Hows, Whys, and Whens down a bit—they don't say anything about what Spear and his followers may have believed or felt about their Mechanical Savior.

This was, after all, a tale about Faith, how it started the entire endeavor of the New Motor...and how she destroyed it.

GUERNICA

By the flatscreen on the wall, it was just past the 21st century. Glowing numerals flickered into 13:00—late enough for the mischief-makers. The cops were still rolling through the city outside, but just maybe a bit lethargically; reptiles chocked full of donuts and acid coffee. The bribes to the neighbors were paid and the acoustics, as always, were perfect—the people on Wake Street hoped.

13:01 and the little house on Wake Street changed. Tension sang through the building; time to play. Outside, the forces of legislated morality motored about—but here, inside, out came the toys. The crowd's change was hard, precise: slaves shrugged off civilian personas and dropped their eyes as masters closed steel-gray attitudes over theirs. The private home with eyebolts, heavily upholstered chairs and mysterious trunks changed: chains were hung, and straps of nasty leather were clipped to tables.

The trunks revealed their contents: highly illegal latex, rubber, dildoes, lubricant, handcuffs, whips, clothespins, canes, condoms, dams, gloves, and other toys. The clock was at 13:15—and then it blipped right over to a tape: Mistress Gloria flagellating a slave. His bedsheet-white ass was striped, welts like red-hot prison bars across his cheeks. He smiled back to the crowd from the screen and a past when he wasn't a criminal, and what he was doing wasn't a Morality Crime. Now, in this year, his stripes could land his ass in jail, or in one of the mining camps, and just viewing the tape could do the same to the people in the Wake Street house.

The cane in the video mistress's hand descended. It was a good quality copy; you could see the slight curve of the white birch rod as it bent to the slope of the slave's ass, the subtle breath of its passing, and the slightly wet kiss of wood to—was that blood? Were those streaks redder than usual welts? Did that rod suddenly have a lipstick streak of the bottom's liquid contents? A very good video. Forget jail, owning this was a one-way ticket to gray hair and hard labor—if you survived interrogation—and all of the pain nonnegotiated, not consensual.

The bottom on the screen became a metronome to the proceedings. *Whack!* Street clothes were put away, play clothes came out. *Whack!* Sudden glimpses of sweat-glimmering thighs, breasts, backs, cheeks, tight chests, chalky skin (the sun never properly introduced to these regions: nudity = jail). *Whack!* A redhead with ribs in evidence and breasts that would rattle in a cupped hand, bent to pull on regulation boots, her sex flowering open behind her and triggering a chorus of salivation from the opposite side of the room. *Whack!* A buzz-cut he-man tugged on regulation prison sweats, the neck and head of his cock vanishing past the drawstrings with a rubbery nod. Those on that side of the room returned the nod, smiling. A comfortable man with a warm, soft chest buckled on his official web belt and pinned a fake badge to his shirt. His eyes followed, with a tightening and flexing of his ass, a short man with tumbleweed-wild hair, who absently tightened and flexed his gloves.

Enforcement Officers patrolled the city outside: tight beams of searing light punching visibility in the darkness, always, perpetually, without sleep (for their sign was a wide-awake, watchful eye) searching for crime, theft, murder, vandalism, vagrancy, ill morality, perversion, homosexuality, sex, affection or enjoyment—less or more than nuclear familiarity.

The clock was still gone, still replaced by the prison-bar-streaked submissive, but they all knew, felt, that it was time to start. Two lines, submissives on one side—quaking in their thin-soled prison shoes (copied with great care from the real thing) against one wall, dominants on the other—flexing leather gloves or fondling toys (copied with great care from the real things, used by those that patrolled outside). The clock couldn't show it, but they all knew it was party time—time to arrest and be arrested by the forces of fear and punishment—ah, but safely, *consensually*.

Some of the submissives had their ankles chained, the links making heavy music on the hardwood floor. The excitement level in the room rose a few notches, and following right behind was a darkside excitement; maybe someone would hear, maybe someone would call the cops, maybe they'd spend the rest of their lives in chains, maybe they'd be beaten, probably they'd die. The fear made simple play into terror play.

There was some hesitancy on the part of the dominants. A spice of suspense for the submissives? No one wanting to start? What was that noise outside?

Then Officer George approached prisoner #16 (Caucasian male, 25-28 years old, brown curly hair cut short, no tattoos or scars). Hooking a sausage finger into a convenient D-ring, the officer hauled the prisoner to his knees and pressed #16's face hard into the leather resistance of his government issued (a copy) crotchguard. "Breathe," he commanded.

The submissive did as instructed, breath squeaking through leather-pressed nostrils.

"Bet it's getting hard," growled the fascist pretender.

The submissive nodded, rubbing his nose (his breathing changed tone) on the hard leather.

Then the officer pulled a pair of handcuffs from his belt, ratcheted them on #16's wrist and then to his own belt. Then he did it again, with another pair of cuffs, another wrist, the other side of the belt.

"How strong are your teeth?" Officer George growled.

#16 dug out the zipper with his lips and teeth and feasted on the condomed cock he found hard and waiting.

A portrait of Officer Lawrence hard at work (done in hard Weegee light, high contrast, gritty, realistic—the untied shoelace, the pistol hanging obviously in the way, the dusty floor, the plaster wall scarred and dented). It'd taken him a few minutes to get into position. And the same went for the target: Lawrence's feet were apart, his arm was back, his fist was clenched, his knuckles were white, his shirt was sweat-stained, his face strained, and his eyes gleamed with feverish concentration.

The whip in his hand was obviously heavy. His wrist was hurting—you could see it in his eyes.

The target was just something officer Lawrence could hit. It wasn't important—just a bull's-eye in felt marker on a pimpled asscheek, that usual ecstatic glazed expression, those runs of welts—they'd all seen his like a thousand times before.

It was the joy Lawrence obviously put into his job that made the picture special.

The body-cavity search Officer Laura was conducting was going well. So far she'd been able to remove the thirty-five cents (two dimes, ten pennies, one nickel) from prisoner #3's ass without having to resort to the enema nozzle hanging next to prisoner #8, Tayle, Sally Q.

That didn't mean, though, that she wouldn't need it eventually.

Officer Goby interrogated prisoner #12:

"What kind of animal are you?"

"I'm a fuck-beast sir."

"What the fuck's that?"

"I live to get screwed, sir."

"Get screwed by what, cunt?"

"Anything that moves, sir."

"Well, I'm not goin' ta fuck ya."

"You're not, sir?"

"You're buttfuck ugly, I don't fuck shit that's buttfuck ugly."

"Am I ugly, sir?"

"Ugly as shit. Why'd you come here, anyway?"

"To get fucked, sir."

"Well you ain't gonna get fucked—too buttfuck ugly. I don't fuck buttfuck ugly."

"What do you with ugly, sir?"

"I beat the crap out of it."

And so officer's belt met transvestite's pantied ass—and Officer Goby's hitting was really pretty—not buttfuck ugly, not at all.

Prisoner #2 was a vaporous man, all pale skin and blue veins, standing, shivering, in one corner. He was an alabaster rail, a naked beanpole.

Officer Eigan was bold, bearded and hairy: a golden bear from some technological forest—adept with the hypodermic, ampules, scalpels, and razors he absently fondled.

...And in one corner a soft, slow (like the slowly menacing gears of some great machine) gang bang was going on—the sex of the lust object in it was lost to conjecture and distant memory.

...On a sling a female prisoner had her pubic hygiene inspected by an iron-plated dyke, the clamps and chains on her tits making a windchime backup to her moaning.

...In a corner two bad boys roughhoused themselves into a squishing doggie-style fuck.

...Tied to the points of the compass on the floor, a knotted prisoner's ass slowly ripened under the constant beating four officers gave it with cane, cat, paddle, and whip (in that order).

...Spread over a vaulting horse, a great-titted redhead cried tears of near-orgasmic joy at the skilled licks of her tiny-titted partner.

...From an iron-barred cage an electronic buzzing and the sting of ozone filled the air—the ongoing torture of a soft, pale prisoner for not doing an adequate Gene Kelly impression. A jolt of current came to his nipples and scrotum with every criticism of his very lackluster soft-shoe.

...One couple, he with a cock, she with a cunt, plugged into each other with a feverish abandon while each, sporting hi-tech claws, painted the other with stripes of slowly drippng blood.

And so on, and on, and on into the night. The clock never moved from the prison-barred ass (but by this time the VCD had been played a half-dozen times) but dawn was threatening nonetheless.

Camp was broken, toys put away, uniforms balled up (or anally folded to regulation standards in the case of those that had gone deep into character), deep breaths taken, nerves steadied, thanks given and taken, dates made, coats buttoned—and out they went.

And, to a player, a distant, predictable thought crossed their minds like a faraway mental freight train: that beyond the front door, down the street, on the corner, at work, at their homes, could wait the crisp precision of an arrest. Prison. The Camps. Death.

They left—excited beyond any play they had done, could do—into *real* terror.

HACKWORK

Hit her, he said, his voice an inch from my ear, inside my skull: *Hit her now.*

The crop didn't feel like much, to me, but I knew it felt more real to him—wherever he was.

Hit her, damnit, his anger copper, his anger stars and then, FIRST WARNING scrolled by my eyesight, just outside my peripheral vision, sent straight into my optic nerve.

The crop was light, almost not in my hand at all. She was on the bed, on her stomach, ass ripe and full, plump and smooth—all but steaming with excitement, already flexing and releasing in preparation.

Hit her now!

✳

It wasn't my first, but I remember that one very well—better than all the others.

I was in New Orleans, dumped after my last fare's money ran out. I'd been stuck in a dingy French Quarter apartment with a lanky, white trash asshole, a Bible-Belt gigolo, his body greasy and alternately sagging and hard as rock as he fucked me. When I'd felt my fare start to come, ghostly quavers flickering up and down my spine and a phantom tightness in the crotch and balls I could feel but didn't have, I'd braced myself—predicting the fare to be a cheap bastard. Too true: as he came, he went—clipping the connection as his cock, wherever it was, started to spurt. As he did, and his ghostly cock and balls vanished from my senses, I pushed the gigolo off and got as far away from his horribly bleached and spotted body—his sagging gut and his crooked, spotted, cock—as I could.

I ignored his baritone complaints—a mix of locally mangled English, Spanish, and Japanese spiced with a Tourette's syndrome of *fucks*, *bitch*es, and *motherfuckers* at not being able to show his "good fine loving" to me, "the pretty lady"—to claim my clothes, efficiently climb back into them and leave, as fast as possible.

The day was pounding hot, the kind of sauna only New Orleans could be. I swam, struggling for breath, till I came to the first cable bar I could find that didn't look like either a trap or too fucking expensive. In the back I found a lonely booth, paid the attendant—a piebald mulatto Korean kid with a cheap Russian prosthetic hand—and located the unit. Sliding my thumb over the id window, I charged up an hour of Blissful Oblivion followed by a chaser of Soulful Self-Examination.

Too soon, the lights of heaven faded, the angels put away their instruments, and the clouds broke up behind my eyes. Then I felt my eyes roll back and I stared hard into my soul.

It wasn't a bad job. I've heard of worse, god knows: horror stories marionettes and jockeys have told me, sitting around company shops waiting for upgrades and maintenance, of wetfun, thrillkills, near-deaths, and even babywipes. Compared to being released from a job in a box apartment somewhere with blood sticking everything to everything else (copper scent too strong in your nose) and half a face on the bed, being a simple hired hack was a good job.

Blame the "elegant facial structure" (as it says on my vid catalog entry), the "piercing blue eyes," "clean," "36-25-36," "long blond hair" and "fully compatible" but I hadn't had a day to myself, as myself, for almost three months. I was popular. I was busy, and I wasn't myself—most of the time.

When I was in the right mood, when I picked Sarcastic Self-Assessment rather than Soulful Self-Examination, I would say that I didn't really know who Rosselyn Moss was anymore—or just who was in the back seat, screaming out directions.

※

The fare came on later that night, as I was stretched out in yet another room, in yet another coffin hotel. They all become one, after a point: the broken telephone in Tokyo, the broken vid in London, the smelly mattress in Seoul. All of them floated and combined to form one fuzzy box: a place to wait, and wait, till someone told me what to do.

Dispatch flickered the FARE WAITING yellow and black status bar across my eyesight, covering the static-fuzzy and rolling image of a local religious zealot spraying spittle as he and his topless "nun" begged for donations.

Then, the words. I had actually started to dream them—their tones warbling and waiving as I flew through dreamscapes, even rented ones, warning me that soon, very soon, I wouldn't be my own man anymore:

Thank you for selecting Express Taxi™ service, the premier service for high class, quality, personal escorts. In just a few moments you will be connected to one of our expert and highly trained taxi personnel. You may feel some disorientation as your nervous system matches with our relay service. If you experience any form of discomfort, or nausea, please summon the assistance of one of our monitors by patting your stomach twice.

Please stand by while we interface with your bio-mate transmission system. Thank you again for selecting Express Taxi™ and we hope you have a pleasant trip!

Interface: the "falling over," the clean, crisp, disorientation as the fare matches with me, shakes hands with my cortical shunts and bioplast sensory nodes.

Then, just like that, I didn't feel quite like *myself*—my senses had been subverted, processed, compressed by black magic algorithms, zapped via the mono-wire antenna that

ran along my spine to the nearest uplink and then to...wher-
ever the fare was, laying back and enjoying the scratchy
mattress, the chill of the box's air conditioning, and the slight
cramp in my leg.

I got a little feedback from him, just enough to tell me
that he was, indeed, a "he," that he wasn't so short or tall as
to screw up my balance—he got most of it, most of what I was
feeling, tasting, seeing, hearing, smelling. From what I could
figure, stretching myself with my usual series of slight exer-
cises to orient him to my body's sensations—the way I feel
things as opposed to the way he felt things—he was about my
height, and near enough to my weight. Once again I felt the
phantom sensation of a cock and balls. You can get used to
anything, I suppose. Walking was the hardest part: try putting
one leg in front of the other sometime with a heavy and
meaty sausage and meatballs between your legs (when you
weren't born with them). Took me months of practice to move
without waddling like a damned duck.

When I was sure that he was comfortably settled in, riding my senses piggyback, I introduced myself, as rote and
familiar as brushing my teeth or tying my shoes: "Good
evening, Sir," I said to myself in the spacious confines of my
pay-by-the-day aluminum coffin, my ears replaying the words
to him. "My name is Rosselyn Moss, your taxi for this trip. I am
a thirty-five-year-old biological female in top physical condition, with no aches or pains that you need be aware of. May I
ask your name, Sir?"

*Go to twelve-thirteen Flood Street, immediately. Take a cab, don't
waste any time.* British accent poured thinly over somewhere
else, somewhere Eastern Europe, German, Russia: "immediately" and "Flood" sounding fluid and bubbling.

I'd become used to the cheap, for whom time is really
money. I knew the drill, I knew the man: yet another vicarious
fuck, yet another nameless pickup so he could feel it like a

woman, me, felt it— at least, that's what I thought.

I was wrong.

Be efficient, he added as I climbed out of my box, *I know this town. I know the way.*

Outside, the night was hot and sticky, a blanket wrapped around me—the day's legacy. People moved through it like underwater ferns and fish. I knew it must have been bad, sweltering, for me to feel it. My fare, though, must have felt it like a steam bath.

He wasn't new at being a taxi fare, so I didn't bother to warn him about the markups on my expenses. I just walked out into the hard sodium lights and to the nearest call box and swiped my card. *Pay for a rush*, he said.

"Yes, Sir," I said. "What, may I ask, is to be your pleasure tonight?"

He didn't respond so I leaned against the side of the call box in the heavy, hot, New Orleans night, and waited.

Hey, what did I care? My meter was running....

❋

She was beautiful. Stretched out on her huge bed, a midnight expanse that all but filled her bedroom, she looked up at me with huge, earthen eyes—lit by quivering desire, a pulse-pounding fever.

Her mouth was on my right nipple, painting it with the gleam of her wet lips, making it harden almost to the point of pain. I felt the ghostly nipping of her white, white teeth. Then she really sucked, and I felt my legs turn to rubber and my cunt get heavy, wet and hot.

In my hand, the crop was light, all but intangible.

❋

We took a table near the back, in the soft shadows where the industrial lights around the stage didn't reach. There was a red biolight in the center of the diamond plate tabletop, making it an island of rich blood. On the stage, a woman was cutting herself with a utility knife, sliding it in diagonal slices across her thin, boyish body. Even in the back, in the shadows of our ruby island, I could see the blackness of her blood dot, then streak, down her belly, waist, and thighs. Cutting and bleeding, she sang a meaningless song, canting her head back to rumble out a random handful of notes, a jumble of half-tunes, mostly lost above the chatting, drinking and laughing crowd.

We'd paid at the door, giving my card to a heavily modified doorman—his face all clear plastic to best show off the geometries of the circuits running underneath—then entered, pausing inside just long enough for my eyes to dilate against the shadows and the sanguine biolights.

To the bar. You can see well enough now.

"Sir," I said, "I do not know if you have been informed or not, but the consumption of consciousness modifiers of any form violates the terms of my hire—"

Not drink, just go.

I went up to the bartender, a giant black man whose skin was much too glossy and thick to be organic, who held his stare at me longer than usual when he saw the taxi mark on my forehead—used to hacks and having to wait till the fare gave the orders.

Ask for a crop. "I want a crop, please."

He smiled, showing teeth capped by .22 bullets, a tongue the color of tire rubber, and brought out a plastic and nylon riding crop.

Longer, smaller tip. I repeated my fare's instructions. As the bartender brought out another, I noticed his eyes were a brilliant red, as if filled with blood or wine.

Pay him. I did. He swiped my card with cool reflexes.

Take it to a table in the back. I did, and my fare and I sat down to watch the show. Sometimes the woman on stage dropped an octave or two as she cut too deep, or just deep enough.

✳

Her.

There were many—the place was busy: Boys in paint and piercings and nothing else; blond warriors colored in bioglow circuits, primitive glyphs and signets. Men roped with amplifier cords, their glandular immenseness augmented by the matte coils. Girls whose bodies vanished and appeared in slices, from their fashionably designed industrial plastic dresses. Women with anger-lit eyes, prowling the club and scratching the steel-plate walls with their charged nails, leaving cascades of sparks and a machine-shop howl.

Her. The black one, in the simple dress. Hair up. Choker of floptical cable, diamond-flashing eyes. The one that looks scared.

She did look that way, hunted eyes scanning—trying not to make contact with anyone else's. She looked like she was caught, trapped, like the whole nightmare club had descended on her. She'd just been walking home and the place had fallen on her. Despite the fevered movements of her head, though, she didn't once step towards the door, towards EXIT.

I timed it just right: when she turned I caught her eye, gestured her toward our table.

Her.

I guess I was a lot less frightening than the others—outwardly. Inwardly, my fare was calm, patient; I didn't get anything from him but the dully flashing HIRED indicator just outside my range of normal vision.

She sat down, smiled with a flash a pure white teeth, and didn't say a word.

Ask her what she's doing here.

I tapped the taxi mark on my forehead, the tattoo that meant that I wasn't my own person and that my words, too often, were not my own. "What are you doing here?"

She shrugged. Her hair was curly, close-cropped dreads penned by a tight band of dimly glowing fabric, its soft blue light making her face appear to be hovering, immaterial, above her black-clothed, black body. "I was curious," she said, with a taste of a Southern accent, though not so strong as to peg her as being local, off the streets. "I heard about it from a friend. She told me some things. I wanted to see for myself."

Put the crop on the table. Ask her if she knows what it means.

I did as he told me, as I was hired to do. "Do you know what this means?"

"I do. I know what it means."

Does she really? "Do you really?"

"I do. I've been told. I want to."

Take her someplace. Hers if it's closer.

"Do you want to go someplace?"

Nein! The voice, the force of it almost like a hard slap behind my ear, in my skull. *Do not ask, tell her. Say to her "We are going now." Do it!*

She had seen the look of shock cross my face. She waited, patiently.

"We're going someplace. Now."

Better—

✾

Hers was closer, a tiny apartment four blocks away. I had gotten maybe twenty feet away from the unnamed club when he said *Come up from behind her, take her wrists and put them behind her back. Do it!*

"Sir, it is against—"

Nein! Do you not understand yet? This is foreplay, this is before— do as I say or I will complain.

I did what I was hired to do. I reached over and grabbed her right wrist, put it behind her back, then her left. It was clumsy, with the crop still in my hand, but I managed—thinking more of the act of juggling the nylon and plastic than of what I was going to do, might end up doing. She leaned back, into me, shocked by the move, the force (though I had been as gentle as possible), and tilted her head back.

Kiss her.

Wine, a tiny trace of garlic. Her tongue was strong, wrestling with mine. Her lips were fat and full.

I broke when he told me to, said "Fucking slut," when he told me to, and pushed her, hard, back down the street. She turned, flattening herself against an ancient brick wall—fear lighting her eyes.

I felt nausea boil in my guts.

Where? "Where?" I echoed, feeling my mind fall into the groove, retreat from my connection with what was going on. It wasn't a technical thing—I just didn't want to be there anymore, didn't want to be a part of what was bubbling up. I did as I was told: following her to her place, waiting while she scanned her thumb, climbing the steep steps with her, going inside.

The place was dark, so she clicked on a biolight that ringed her bedroom. A huge, black, wrought iron bed. A Christ against the wall, also huge—looking like it might have fallen off some church, sadly watching over her bed.

He said, I did: grabbing her shoulder and turning her so that she faced away from me. He said, I did: putting my hand over her mouth, cupping it as I bit down into the thick muscles of the back of her neck.

He said, and, yes, I did: taking hold of the dress and pulling, hard, hearing and seeing the cloth tear all the way down to her ankles.

Throw her on the bed.

Her back was hot, like a pot left on the fire. I shoved, feeling myself pull back at the last, resist the feeling to shove her really hard, really *throw* her onto her expanse of black sheets, and wrought iron.

Turning, she looked back over her shoulder at me like a wild animal hearing the hunter thrash through the brush. She was gorgeous, body full and rich; rounded at ass, thighs and breasts, poured, overflowing, into purple bra, garters, hose. No panties, just a black fog of curly hair.

His voice, thundering:

Hit her.

✻

Nein, wait, first—take her ankles, pull her toward you. Idiot! Put the crop down first, on the bed. Yes! Pull her toward you. Good, now turn her over, hard. Do it, idiot! Yes, yes—such a pretty cunt she has: such a pretty, pretty cunt. So black. She gleams, ja? She shines for us, for me. Tell her, speak to her, tell her she is wet. Tell her that she is a cunt, just a pussy for us. Tell her.

The words jammed in my throat and I stammered, but they came. I felt my body break sweat from my feet to my face, a fever of fear and disgust that made everything waver in the hot room. I wanted to drop away, to give up completely and just let him have me, do what he wanted to do with her. I just didn't want to watch anymore.

But I didn't think, not once, of cutting the connection. *Take off your blouse, take off your bra—I know your nipples are hard because I can feel them. Do nothing, do not say anything. Just stand.*

I do. She turns quick and wraps her lips around my right nipple, sucking with her strong lips, teasing it with her strong teeth. One hand, her right, reaches up to tickle my left.

Take her hair, force her back.

I do, drawing her off my nipple. Then she's free, panting like she'd been running, eyes fixed on, first, crinkled, hard, nipple and then, second, my face.

Draw her up, pull her up by her hair. Do it!

I lifted her by her hair with one hand and, with the other, her chin. She helped by climbing up onto her knees. Then she was kneeling in front of me. A nipple (like a drop of coal on her breast), I saw, mesmerized, had fallen free of her bra.

Tear it off.

I did, my arms following his directions—my mind disconnected, retreated into doing exactly what he said to do.

Her breasts were lovely and dark; large but not fat, bigger than mine—they barely fell as the bra snapped and tore in my hands (she almost falling forward by my earnest ripping). Two nipples out, then, both large and hard, blacker on black.

Tell her that if she makes a sound or moves away the game is over and we will leave. Tell her—

I do, his words falling from my mouth.

Take her nipples in your hands, thumbs and forefingers, and squeeze. Hard! Harder than that—you idiot, this is what she's here for. Do it!

I think about reminding him of our contract, that I could make a case for cutting him for abusive treatment of me. I don't, though. I don't. I couldn't say a word, I just took her nipples and captured them in my hot and sweaty hands (dimly aware of his cock, a phantom ache of hardness somewhere) and squeezed as hard as I could.

Her eyes got wide. Her breath came hot and heavy, like a horse's after a race, sweat making her reflect the dim green light in the room—polishing her with pain and something else. I was aware of her smell, rich and strong, as I watched her widening pupils staring at me (at me?)—black walnuts quivering in pure cream.

Run your fingers through her cunt, get her juice on your fingertips. Hold them in front of her face. Say, "This is what you are."

I did, my body did—my mind in the back, shaking with fear and something else. She sucked my fingers, tasting herself and growling in heat.

Take her, turn her hard and throw her on the bed.

I did. Her ass was tight, hot, and glimmering on the bed. Her smell was even stronger. She rose up on all fours, the perfect globes of her ass parting, showing me herself, offering herself to me.

Hit her.

I held the crop and did not move, trapped between his bellowing voice and my own arm. I only do what he says I have to do. He does not have control. I will break the connection, pull myself in, zip myself up and leave.

I will.

Coward. You are afraid. Gott, you feel it, but you are scared. She wants this, she needs this as much as I do. She wants the crop, idiot. She wants to feel your force, your power. That is why she is here, why I am here. Do it now, fool, or I will break and report you: we do this because we want to do this. I take nothing that is not offered.

Look at her, she wants it more than your body. Hit her, damn you, hit her and give us what we both want!

Anger was a vibrating wire in my guts, around my spine. The crop was light in my hand—but I knew he felt it more than I did, my senses rerouted to my fare.

Hit her now! His anger was an echoing copper taste in my mouth. He must have complained, VRslanged with one hand to transmit his dissatisfaction to Dispatch because FIRST WARNING scrolled by. Hacks were allowed only two. Anger. At him, her, or me I didn't know then, don't even know now. I hit her, clumsy and inaccurate.

Good—but aim better, hit her light at first, get her used to your hand, the toy. Tap her. Aim for the sugar spot, there—between her tailbone and the top of her thigh, parallel with her cunt. There. Hit her there.

I did, my hand light at first but with growing frustration and anger (him, her, me, him, her, me). Soon my hand and the crop were a vibrant blur, its plastic tip slapping on her rich black ass. She quivered and shook, moaned and jumped. She made noises no lover before or since has made for me, or any of my fares.

She leaned back to get closer to each blow, then jumped forward at the crack of it. Flexing, knotting her magnificent black ass, she echoed the impact with the clenching of her muscles: her thighs, her cunt.

Good, good! Now you understand. Feed her the crop, use it to make her moan and beg, cry and scream! Use it: Make it hard and fast and mean! Yes!

His cock was hard, a ghostly ache that I couldn't touch—somewhere—distantly, shamefully, I knew my own cunt was steaming, aching to be touched, licked, satisfied.

The crop went from a blur to a humming WHACK! as I used it—faster and harder, harder and faster—more and more. She wasn't just moaning, towards the end, she was crying and screaming with each sharp impact.

Then: *Fuck her.*

I didn't have a real one, and his was wherever he was, but I knew and he knew exactly what he meant. I climbed up on the bed and sank my right hand into her—feeling the burning heat of her ass, the furnace of her cunt with first one, then two, then three, then four fingers. It was only an aftermath, though, and he came as she came, from something our quick fist couldn't touch: the whip.

Then he was gone, pulled out and away. AVAILABLE flashed across my vision.

She was quivering, shaking from the crop and, maybe, from my hand—just a little. Sadness dropped over me and I felt like crying. Her ass was burning, so hot from the beating we—no, I—had given her. She didn't seem able to relax. Even as I wiped my hand of her wetness, carefully pulled the bedclothes up and over her, and put a pillow under her loose-rolling head she jumped and quivered still from the crop.

I tucked her in and kissed her forehead. Her face seemed to be on fire and her breath was quick and hot. I wanted to cry, the tears heavy in my eyes making the room seem submerged.

I went to leave then but she called from the bed, a small voice. I went over to her, knelt down and said, "Sorry?"

Then she said: "Call me. Please. Call me."

I smiled, and patted her head, almost, almost saying I would but then I knew, totally, then and there, that she didn't mean me, didn't mean Moss.

She meant *him*.

HEARTBREAKER

Lies are bad for you, Kusa thought, looking at the place through her bulletproof sunglasses. Eat you up from the inside, they will, chew you up till there's nothing left—nothing true, at least.

I should know, she added to herself with a wry smile—or at least as much of one as her customized exoskeletal system would allow. It was good but there were always things that were a bit too subtle for polyplastics, ceramics, and mnemonic alloys.

I should know: Not much that's true about me, anymore.

The building was so skillfully trashed that it had to be camouflage. Just the right amount of empty syringes, roaming-gang tribal graffiti, bubble-pack, synth-meat containers, and air-freight shipping cocoons. To eyes (all right—lenses) used to deception, the smell of rotting garbage, urine, ozone, and blood was too well orchestrated, too finely assembled to be real. Even in the bad parts of a bad town this was too bad.

It was an urban skull and crossbones: a city DO NOT DISTURB.

They'd had the place staked for almost two weeks now, and their taps, long-ears, scopes, monitors, and flea-bugs had all told them the same story, over and over again: pay dirt.

Every other unit would have gone right in, busted it flat, made a couple of hot collars, had their faces splashed on the newsnet, and rested on their asses for a good month—high on glory and departmental commendations.

But a word had been whispered during those two weeks, and Kusa had been lucky to hear of it. Faster than the SWAT team, her M-2 unit was on-site and in control. Sure, the beat cops, the undercovers, vice, and the rest of them had screamed, stamped their little feet, cried their professional tears and threatened to have their big, bad captain rip her a new asshole. Till, that is, she'd shown them the commissioner's ID on their orders, her sternest polyplastic glower (one emotion easily carried by her exoskeleton), and the flash-suppression muzzle of her favorite Vesper automag—not necessarily in that order. In the space of twenty minutes the Musani police were gone and M-2 were in charge of the operation.

Heartbreaker.

44 Noyama Street was a mini-warehouse in a long parade of same, a row of prefabricated dominoes that had long ago fallen economically. If she wanted to, she knew she could look down the street and see where one of them was gutted from a long-forgotten fire, another had been converted to a cheap hooker dive, and yet another was clogged with fever-vine—a bio-organic factory that had gone out of control. Aside from the careful application of crap, 44 was just one of its down-trodden and crapped-out kin.

Kusa moved carefully to the side alley. The front of 44 faced the street: mouth a huge industrial roller-door, eyes two dirt-opaqued windows, nose a small vent leaking steam. The side alley was carefully choked with garbage—except for a narrow path that led to a steel-clad door.

Heartbreaker. In the language of cops the word meant drugs, puppets, illegal stims, stolen memories and, the rumors whispered, a little chemical slavery. Some thought that the word was a group name, a front for a syndicate, a gang, or an urban tribe. Others thought that it was just a code word for an activity, for a preference, for more sinful, carnal crimes.

The door was smeared with paint, industrial binding gel, and something Kusa really didn't want to guess at. It didn't look like it had a peephole. Solid steel. But she'd been scanned at least half a dozen different ways just walking down the alley: microwaves, millimeter-wave radar, and even ultrasound.

"Yes?" The voice was stripped by electronics of everything save content. Old? Young? Female? Male? All Kusa could tell, with even her specialized internal detection gear, was that it had said *yes*.

Heartbreaker. She could sense him, feel him moving in the background of his chosen crimes. He had a style, a kind of art to his rapes, thefts, and assaults.

She'd also seen him once, back when she was still fairly wet. Tall, thin, blond. He'd been standing outside of a place very similar to 44 Noyama. The unit she'd been assigned to had been lucky—they'd been tipped off to a major haul of puppetware. They arrived just in time to see him, standing there.

She didn't have time to make a good scan to see if he'd been modified or was flesh and blood. Kusa didn't have time because he had stood there, calmly, smiling, before transmitting a barrow-beam signal that had tripped the five pounds of gel Plastique hidden in the building. Kusa had lost her right arm and left leg in the blast and four others of her team had been flatlined.

Yes, the door had said.

"Someone told me to come," Kusa answered, letting her on-board inflection circuits clear any trace of the lie from her voice.

"Fuck off. You don't have a fucking appointment."

"Said I didn't need one if I brought enough."

The door silently swung inwards, showing nothing but darkness.

"You'd better have," the voice said as Kusa stepped inside.

Vines embraced industrial struts. Flowers like smiling faces glowed with delicious colors. The floor was covered with a spongy mat of dead leaves, a cushioned mulch that felt like industrial rubber. Sunlight leaked in through the two upper story windows: narrow beams of hard white that trapped small insects and lots and lots of wheeling constellations of dust.

Kusa was struck dumb.

"You like our garden?"

The walls were lost to the jungle. Pencils, cables, telephone poles—the plants seemed to come in all shapes and thicknesses. One monster looped up and around the interior space, surrounding them with a brilliant green corkscrew. It must have been two meters across. Other vines were like a fine mist, dancing in the turgid, humid breeze that rolled through the room like an ocean swell.

The building, according to the specs they'd pulled out of the developer's database, was only ten meters by twenty. Kusa stood in the middle of a rain forest, an interior jungle in the middle of an old industrial park. It seemed to go on forever.

"I didn't come to pick berries," Kusa said, scanning the deep green for the owner of the voice. Despite her training, and the cop software riding her hind brain, she had to keep the soft oscillations of awe out of her voice.

"No impressing some people," the voice said again, but this time her on-board processors had enough of the real voice to break the distortion down: female. "Lot of it's real, of course—genesliced and tinkered with. Some of our...customers can't really pay on the net, so they lend their talents to our garden. A little recombinant engineering here, a little nanomech there. The walls are behind holocover of course—the room ain't that big."

Female, positive. 21-25 years of age. No evidence of inhalant drugs. Education: superior—more than likely upper college educated or a self-taught education-hacker. Taki, her backup, whispered: *Probably a good part of the operation. Knock her off her perch and we'll try and get a trace on anything leaving the area—she'll have to ask the boss for advice,* directly into her neural interface. Because of the possibility of counter-bugs, the feed

was direct and very strong: Kusa could just about feel her partner sitting in their undercover van up the street, jacked into
her feed. Taki was a hovering godhead in the back of her
mind, watching, criticizing, all-knowing and—if she needed
it—the thrower of thunderbolts.

"I came to make a deal," Kusa said, calling into the real
and artificial jungle, at the same time blipping back a coded
confirmation signal to Taki.

"How special." The voice was subtly laced with a soft
laugh. "Two steps forward, then two right, then two forward."

Vines parted like a curtain, some when she touched them,
others seemed to predict her movements and softly pulled
themselves out of her way. The directions seemed too brief for
the huge jungle, and she honestly expected more—twenty
steps? Fifty?—but then she was in the clearing.

The Amazon suddenly fell away. It was as if she had
entered a bubble of clarity in a vibrant green fog of plants. The
floor was still hidden by a dense and chaotic mat of vines and
roots, but the rest of the space was clear for about six meters
in any direction. The jungle had been dim and dark, but the
clearing was perfectly placed where a beam of sunlight
landed from the high windows.

In the middle was a wrought-iron four-poster bed, an art
nouveau imitation of the jungle vines. Covering the bed was a
fine gauze of mosquito netting (even though she didn't sense
any of the damned bugs).

"What do you consider a deal?" the girl said.

It was hard to pull any details out of her, at first, as she
was hidden behind the fuzzing whiteness of the mosquito
netting—and Kusa didn't want to do any active scanning till
she knew more of the electronic layout of the place. Just as
she was about to jump her image amplification, the girl
moved the netting aside and climbed out of the bed—and it
creaked with her weight.

She was young. Correction—when money could make even the ancient fresh again—she was young-looking. Pale, almost translucent, skin. Hair the color of a raging brushfire. Her eyes were too blue: they glowed the color of a cloudless sky—a cosmetic affectation. Her face was the perfect mixture of pale cheeks, button nose, gentle forehead, and shapely neck.

She was nude.

We have a low emission coming from somewhere in the structure. Modulated maser. We don't have a fix on it yet, Taki said from somewhere just above her left ear.

The girl's body was thin, in a kind of arrested pubescent way: small, very pointed breasts topped by small nipples—almost an afterthought. Slight belly, fine legs. She was tight and strong—the perfect muscles of a young girl before gravity and age. She wasn't shaved or creamed: her pubis was faintly hidden by a few brush strokes of brilliant red hairs.

The girl smiled, put pale hands on even paler hips. "Deal?" she reminded Kusa.

"Is the boss around?" Kusa said, shifting her weight to show her indifference to the jungle, the girl.

"I'm around. You talk to me." The girl's eyes lit with fire, with a kind of fierce concentration.

Kusa ached to snap on her actives and give the girl, and the room, a blast of modulated laser light, a drumroll of subsonics, or a pan of deep radar—but she was running silent, running deep. Do that and if there were any kind of sensitives in the room they'd whoop and holler their electronic brains out.

Though not completely flesh and blood, she was still a damned good cop. She didn't need her active electronics to deal with this—she had twenty years behind her. Didn't need polyplastics, a bio-support cradle, or a fucking nanospun framework. She had all she needed in her damned braincase.

Heartbreaker.

"I don't know you," Kusa said to the girl, looking at her

coldly through her sunglasses.

"Well I don't know you either," the girl said with a little laugh, water slipping down a brook.

Kusa had carefully put herself together. She knew the look to go for, knew the things that would cut her some slack with the kind of crowd Heartbreaker hung with. Old military boots, old jump pants, black T that had once advertised a Korean protein drink, bashed and scuffed leather coat, her shades. She'd seen the same look a million times, on the street and on a lineup display.

It had been a long time since Kusa had worn anything save her standard frame—part familiarity with the size and the reactions, part nostalgia. She was still big-boned and tall: she towered over the tiny girl. Her shoulders were wide and her hips were strong. The squad called her BB for Big Bitch.

Could be just housekeeping junk or a direct line to the boss. Cracking is gonna take time. Whatever you're doing, keep it going.

"Ten packs of Might." Might was the street name of Mitrol-D, a stimulant hotly desired by most hired muscle.

The girl smiled again, a very bewitching expression. "You're in the door now."

"Military grade. CS-2." Top of the line. Max dosage and concentration.

The girl's smile lit, and fireworks danced in her eyes. "Can I get you anything? Orange juice?" she said, picking a simple glass tumbler off the floor and moving to a knotted vine. Swiftly untying it, she caught the stream of juice that poured out in the glass.

Kusa accepted it, nodding.

The girl retied the vine and wiped her hands on a huge leaf. "Do you have it on you?"

It was Kusa's turn to smile. "I know where it is."

"I think you're someone I'd like to know," she said, smiling up at Kusa with those pinwheel eyes. Kusa still couldn't tell if she was meat or metal. "Name's Nine."

"Nine?"

"Boss gave it to me, says it's cause I'm just short of a ten—and then only because he decided I needed a dose of humility. Jerk."

"Hirano," Kusa said, using a name their team had skillfully given a perfectly corrupt past and Kusa's face.

"Nice to meet you, Hirano. So how did you score the Might?" Nine walked over to the bed, tied back the mosquito netting and sat down, patting the mattress next to her.

Tentatively, Kusa sat. Nine still came up to about her shoulder, making her feel like she was sharing the bed with a much-younger kid sister. "Someone I know leaned on a Supervisor at Top Guard—leaked it out in a hollow kidney."

"Swift. You been doin' this long?"

"Long enough. Used to run with McGregor and Dobbs."

"Till those M-2 assholes blew them away."

Kusa nodded. McGregor had shot her in the leg and Dobbs had tried to get her with an anti-tank rocket—luckily she had recently upgraded and only spent two days in the shop getting refitted.

Nine put a pale, thin hand on Kusa's shoulder. "You look like someone I should get to know better."

"I'm flattered."

"In some ways you should be, in some ways you shouldn't. My standards are very high, as are the boss's, but I do know a lot of people." Nine's hand gingerly traced a line down Kusa's arm to her hand. Kusa's skin was the best, so even though she still wore her leather jacket, Nine's touch felt like she was stroking her bare arm.

Nine looked up at Kusa, with freshly dancing lights in her eyes. "My, you're a big girl, aren't you?"

It's definitely outgoing, taps into a junction box two blocks away, then into the fibrenet. Probably a direct line to the boss. This is it, BB, this is fucking it. Keep her going while we run a trace on it. It's tough—we're looking at twenty, thirty minutes, tops.

Nine cupped Kusa's firm, hard breast, ran a pale finger across the subtle rise of her nipple through the old T-shirt. "Do you have any problem with me getting to know you better, Hirano?"

"None that I can think of," Kusa said, feeling her nipple wrinkle and harden under Nine's soft stroking. When she'd been rebuilt, Kusa's only change was a concession to form vs. function. She'd had her breasts flattened and strengthened for her new body. Before losing most of her torso in the blast, she'd been almost too big to deal with (they got in the way). Now she was athletic, lean.

Nine cupped the strong, lean tit as if feeling its weight. "You like looking so strong?" she asked, pinching Kusa's nipple.

"Comes in handy."

"Bet it does. Me, I like taking them off guard. Like what you see?" Nine said, smiling her little girl face up at Kusa, brushing imaginary crumbs off her strong thighs, her barely furred mons.

"As a matter of fact, yes I do," Kusa said, smiling back, after Taki blipped into the audio-sensing part of her brain. *Thirty minutes, give us thirty minutes....*

"Take this off," Nine said, tugging at Kusa's jacket.

"What if someone walks in? What if your boss shows up?"

Nine laughed, taking Kusa's jacket and carefully putting it down next to the bed. "He lets me have my fun. I let him have his." Again, Nine cupped Kusa's breast through her T-shirt as if judging its weight. "Very good job," she said.

"Thank you. If you have to live in it, buy the best," Kusa said, as Nine snaked a thin arm up behind her head and drew her down into a kiss.

The kiss was a spark, it lit up the back of Kusa's head like a road-flare in the dark. Almost instantly she felt her body respond—and was so overwhelmed by her quickened breathing, tightening nipples, warming skin that she didn't put together the obvious: "You're very fine, too," she said when Nine let go of her long enough for her to snatch a breath. Kusa was big, strong and heavy, yet Nine had pulled her down to her like she was flesh and blood again.

"Thank you," Nine said, tugging at Kusa's shirt "Designed it myself."

Kusa couldn't help laughing a bit. Nine was almost a cartoon of the young girl her body was modeled after—even down to chewing her lip as she struggled to get the tight shirt off. Finally Kusa just reached down and hauled it over her head herself.

"Very pretty," Nine said, instantly latching herself onto Kusa's right nipple with her very strong lips.

Oh, boy—Kusa thought. Nine was ferocious. If her nipples weren't artificial she was sure she would have yelped with surprise and pain. As it was, the pleasure tips in her nipples surged with delightful sensation till they almost reached a shrieking volume.

"Careful now," Kusa said, patting the back of Nine's head, "or they'll come off."

"Can't believe someone so tasty would ever buy something so shoddy—you just need some more warm-up, is all."

Nine's lips felt like silk. Kusa's could distinguish some thousand or so sensations (top of the line, man): packed with almost ten thousand nanotech receptors, her lips could tell the difference between Swiss or California chocolate just by the consistency. Nine's lips were silk. Fine grade, tight weave, hand-washed, *silk*.

Their kiss seemed to last ages—tongues rolling hot and fluid with each other. Neither of them breathed, so it seemed as if they were both submerged in a surging bath of warmth. Kusa felt her cunt start to boil. She found her big hands all but involuntarily cupping Nine's tiny tits, stroking her childlike nipples and feeling them also bud-up with her excitement.

Didn't need to, but it was still a nice perk: Kusa's nose could distinguish between over three dozen types of plastic explosive and a hundred different kinds of coffee. She could smell if a gun had been fired within the last week and follow certain biologics by the smell of their fear. Nine didn't need to smell, didn't need to have any kind of aroma—save the clean-child smell she affected as part of her whole package—but it was nice, nonetheless. As they kissed, locked and boiling together, Kusa definitely caught the pure smell of Nine's excitement rising from her own re-engineered cunt.

"Nice touch. Wasn't an option I went for," Kusa said, breaking the kiss.

"But I bet you've got some fun options, too—somewhere else maybe." Nine smiled back, pinching Kusa's left nipple very, very hard between a strong thumb and forefinger.

The sensations that shot from Kusa's nipple and into her brain made her arch her back and moan.

"Oh, I've got some, all right." Nine's nipples were small and pink, hard but still just a kind of punctuation on her small breasts. In Kusa's big, strong hands her breasts, let alone the small nipples, all but vanished. *Don't try this at home, meaties*—she thought, crushing one of Nine's tits in her hand.

Nine's eyes grew wide. Clamping her legs together, she shook her head back and forth. Even though she didn't need to, she breathed hard and quick. Tears started to run down her face.

Nice touch, Kusa thought, changing tits and squeezing even harder.

"Fuck!" squealed Nine, grabbing hold of Kusa's hand. She could probably very easily have pulled even Kusa's rebuilt hand away, but she didn't: she just held on to Kusa like an anchor in a storm.

"You're one mean bitch, aren't you, Hirano?"

"Among other things, yes."

"Well, Ms. Hirano, let's see if you can fuck as well as you can feel," Nine said, jerking Kusa's pants down.

"Only one way to find out." *Getting there, BB. Getting there. Maybe fifteen, maybe twenty. Can you hang on?* Taki said from inside her mind. She blipped back an affirmative, almost adding, *Damned right I can.*

Nine started fondling her own cunt, absently rubbing the tiny red (of course) bead of her clit as she gently started to coax her lips apart.

Kusa was so fascinated by the realism, the fucking pornographic details of Nine's cunt that she almost forgot to get her own ready. Shaking herself out of her hypnotized fascination with Nine, she kicked off her boots, pulled her pants the rest of the way down and off. Then she reached down between her own legs and started to coolly rub her own magic button.

"Gimmie tittie," Nine mumbled, leaning forward to plant her silken lips on Kusa's right nipple again.

Oh boy oh boy—Kusa thought, furiously working her own clit. As the heat of her hand and the heat of Nine's gorgeous body started to work on her, she gently pushed Nine back on the bed—breaking the younger-looking girl's suction on her nipple for just a second.

"AC/DC?" Nine said, licking Kusa's nipple with a long, velvety tongue.

"Microsec 7-80."

"Cool," Nine said, turning Kusa till she was lying down on the comfortable bed. Kneeling down on the floor, Nine kissed her then, there—between Kusa's thighs, at the tiny rift that started near the top of her mons and ended somewhere near her asshole. Kusa liked being human—liked being a woman. She had the option of being something else, when it became more advantageous to just scrap the rest of her blasted, broken, and torn body and stick her cortex in a bio-support cradle. The choices they had offered, those Swiss industrial sculptors: lions, men, children, vehicles, or just a brain in a tank, living off VR sims.

She picked a woman—very similar to her old self. She had liked her old self. She had even kept a close approximation to her old cunt—she had liked her body a lot.

Nine gently parted her cunt lips and gave her clit a tentative lick—

—*getting there, BB. Ten, maybe fifteen. Keep 'em busy*—

—then Nine started to get right down to it. She was very, very good. She had the kind of elegant style to her licks and kisses that said Nine was a girl right down to her own few scraps of original DNA. Men, even men who were now just brains in a mechanical body, never could have licked pussy like Nine did.

After she'd pushed Kusa up that long incline towards the drop-off into a screaming, thrashing come Nine suddenly stopped and kissed Kusa's thighs. Then again she gently parted Kusa's cunt lips and deftly snaked a pale finger into her. The feeling was marvelous for Kusa. The swimming sensation of Nine's finger notched her ride up to orgasm a little further.

Feeling around inside Kusa's cunt, Nine hooked a finger around Kusa's genital interface cable and carefully pulled it out.

"Cool," Nine said, holding the cable while she climbed up onto the bed to lie next to Kusa "—don't even need an adapter."

Side-by-side on the bed they kissed, mixing tongues and heat together. As they did, Kusa became distantly aware of Nine fishing around inside her own wet cunt—the soft sounds of slippery, smacking cunt lips making a nice background sound to their kisses.

"Now for the fun," Nine said, holding up her own cable, lead trailing back to the gleaming seam of her own cunt.

Quickly, with a gentle click of fine engineering, she connected them together.

Fireworks. Explosions. A white-hot surge of a primal force. Wetness. Hardness. A screaming of matching interfaces. The taste of blood and cunt juice. Skin so soft as to be almost unfeelable. Breaths mingling in a blast-furnace kiss. Tongue ballet. Lenses fogging—

Their cunt was on fire, molten; their lips and their clit steamed in a thumping beat as their bodies moved over each other. Nipples stroked across soft breasts, bellies glided on a sheen of fine synthetic sweat. Their cunt was rapidly melting in a pool of vibrating wine, a tub of jiggling butter. They were burning in their roaring lust, combining in an echoing, reverberating bonfire. Linked, each hardwired into the other's genitals, mixed and matched, they surged and merged—

Nine licked Kusa's nipple, and they both felt like they were being licked and doing the licking. Kusa deftly parted Nine's labia and tasted the sea-saltiness of her dripping cunt and felt her own hands part her own lips and kiss and lick her own cunt.

They both felt both their comes start to rise, heavy and thrilling, up their spines.

Soon it rose so far and so fast that the only thing either of them could see was a pale red mist, a muscle-locking tension that shook them like a pleasant seizure. Mixed and mingled, wet and melted together, they came in a chorus of warbling screams.

Panting like spent thoroughbreds, they lay sprawled across each other. Somehow Kusa's leg got wrapped around Nine's thigh and the pale girl seemed to have her mouth permanently affixed to Kusa's right nipple.

—*Got it. Did you copy, BB? We got it, pull out, man—pull out! Got a fix: an old industrial park five klicks from here. Pull out damn it or we're gonna fucking leave you. The line's still hot—*

Kusa mussed Nine's hair, feeling the echoing tension that still sang between them through their jacked cunts. Their diminishing excitement was like a descending note played through both their artificial bodies. "That was wonderful," Kusa said, stroking Nine's mane of fiery hair. "You're busted."

✳

Cuffed by unbreakable plastic shackles, Nine was callously dumped in the back of an unmarked police van. Inside, with cool efficiency, a cop-tech jumped her motor responses with a bypass clip—leaving her a very expensive pile of non-functioning limbs.

She didn't mind.

Isolated in her wetware, her thoughts were bubbling and happy—a giggling spasm of delight and self-satisfaction.

So predictable, Kusa—when I've set out the right bait. Stick your perfect body type, a perfect fantasy, right under your nose and watch you stumble in. You fell right where I wanted you to fall.

Thinking of the special software she'd slipped Kusa in the middle of their fuck, Nine roared with laughter in her mind— thinking of how she'd rewired the M-2 agent's pleasure centers, subtly disconnecting Kusa from her ability to orgasm.

Always the stone-cold cop, Kusa—always one step behind. Bribes beyond you, even bending the rules out of the question. You're the fucking Big Bitch, Kusa, and you're out to get me, aren't you?

But I've got you, BB. I've got you by your short and curlies. Maybe not now, but definitely soon—long after I've ditched this body, you're going to figure it out: No comes, no pleasures—not even a little. Nothing without my little key to unlock your mind. You wanted to be an unfeeling bitch, Kusa—well now you are.

I wonder how long it'll take before you really start to feel that itch you can't scratch, that ache you can never, ever, get rid of.

Maybe then, Kusa, you might be more willing to...listen to reason, Heartbreaker thought as the van pulled quietly away.

SWITCH

Who shall I be tonight?

I don't know ... and never will, anonymity being as much an attraction to them as the body—my body—they rent. They're even spared a simple splinter of recall, a furtive glance from me as they walk in the door. No, my day begins when I enter—passing through the thick glass doors and into the cool darkness of the employees' lounge. You'd think, after the three years that I've been working at the Maison Mirage, that the touch of the machines would have lost its chill—but it hasn't, and the last thing I remember is the prickling of my skin, a cascade of goose bumps, as their examining tendrils and curious probes make sure that I haven't brought something microscopic and unseemly into their elegant palace of dalliances.

The next thing I remember is their touch again—another embrace of fine technology as they make sure I don't take something of the client out into the rest of the world. A flake of skin, a glimmer from a misplaced kiss, a drop of semen—these are as good as a brilliant announcement of my renter, the client who's used me.

If not for the ripple of mental displacement, the slight changes in my body from dawn to dusk, I could easily blur the caresses of the cleaning machines into a single experience—and my life would be walking with sunlight in my face into the elegant foyer of the Maison Mirage, into the cool darkness of the lounge and their microfilament touches, and then out again into the nighttime darkness.

I can never know; the establishment's guarantee sees to

that. Its appeal is to those whose pleasures must remain so secret, so hidden. When I work, so they say, I am not myself—I'm a different self, one that I can never know.

Still, I wonder sometimes—rummaging through guesses picked from absent consumption of men's images—who I am for them.

I wonder, yes, but I know I'll always be theirs. That's the thing that keeps me entering the gentle luxury of the Maison, keeps me returning day after day.

A French Maid perhaps—a ruffle-skirted Fi-Fi with a ridiculous accent and breasts spilling from a constricting bodice. Maybe I would be dusting, merrily humming a song of no import, when the Master enters and—enticed by my swelling femininity—runs a firm hand up my stockinged legs to my simple panties. I would shriek—not from outrage but rather from pleasure—and his questing fingers would find moisture and wild heat. A little later, his cock would be out, a column of thick flesh dotted by a pearl of creamy excitement, and my lips would find it—driven by my lust and commanded by his firm, bass voice. I would become his servant, but not one ordered just to dust his library.

Or maybe a blooming schoolgirl? A ripe young woman in gray skirt and white blouse—bouncing through this fantasy like a sprite dancing through the woods, nipples peaking against the starched brilliance of my blouse, simple cotton panties flashing with each high-kicking stride. I doubt I would be a girl, but rather a just-turned woman. Maybe he'd punish me first, his strong hands whapping firm and unstoppable against my pantied ass, sending shivers of pain and delight through my rich, lusty body. Then, perhaps, he'd bring me into the world of wondrous sexual pleasure, pulling those now damp knickers down around my quaking knees and gently—or not—easing a throbbingly earnest member into my inner recesses. My wetness would surround his pumping cock, dripping down around his fat, hairy balls and the tight crack of my ass. With our mutual orgasms he'd lead me into fantastic realms of sexual pleasure with a strong hand on my ass, and a commanding tone in his voice.

Ah, but why not just a slave girl? A woman trained in the arts of pleasure—supplicant and humble in his mighty presence. I would be brought to him, naked and shimmering with a lotion of constant sexual readiness, my firm body moving as my Keepers had trained me, in order to arouse my new Master. With collar around my neck, I would be presented to him—the treasure he has waited for. There would be a ritual next, I think; a bonding between Master and Slave, a series of powerful acts that would bring us together: he with my leash, me at the end. Maybe with a cane, paddle, or just with his hand he'd warm my ass—maybe with clip, clamp or just his gripping fingers he'd toughen my nipples - maybe with dildo, fingers, or his own mighty cock, he'd fuck the deep, hot, wet depths of my cunt. Whatever the tool, whatever the act, I would be his property, his pleasure, his slave.

Or perhaps his tastes are more earthly, more primal. I close my eyes and see myself as a prostitute of the long-ago ages, a hooker, burned and callous—tired of the world, tired of the John, exhausted from spreading my legs for just one more fuck, one more too-short stack of bills. Chewing gum, eyes dead to pleasure, only alive for money, I would dully call out to his strong visage the mantra of my tired profession: "Wanna date?" Seeing in me something special, something that he could bring back to glorious, passionate life, he accepts my offer and we go upstairs. There, though, he takes me roughly by the hair, throwing me onto my tired brass bed. The frame squeaks and the metal glimmers—perhaps for the first time in many, many years. He explains his desires, offers me a way out. I refuse of course, seeing in him a challenge—a man to break, perhaps just because he stupidly will try and break me.

But there are other possibilities, as many as there might be clients. At night, after my forgotten time at their hands, I close my eyes and try to think of them. My imagination is vivid, but

I know I can only conjure a small fraction of the deep desires. I think of hands slapping my tender ass, making it blush; I think of toys—whips and canes, and all the rest—and the pain, at first, that blasts through my body with each touch, each stroke, each hard impact. I dream of their hands tight around mine—like steel, gripping me. I imagine struggling, but am held too fast in their so-firm grips.

As I'm thinking, my cunt responds—moistening, blooming with feverish desire. Sometimes I slip a finger between my legs and circle the entrance, thinking of those cocks sliding into me, their fat heads pushing my tender flesh aside, delving, pounding hard into me. I think of my juices coating their members with the shine of my lust.

I think, I dream, I wish—but it's not even a memory, because I'm not allowed any. I stretch out on my simple bed, in my simple flat, and spin my wishes of what they might be like, their faces, their rough hands, their cruel implements, their...cocks, in my mouth, in my hands, in my so-wet cunt.

I think, I dream, I wish—but it's all intangible, and so hard to hold on to. But just about every night I spread my legs and dip my fingers between them, stirring my hot juices with stiff fingers. Yes, the hopes and dreams come, but that isn't what pushes me over the top, makes me clamp down on my own hand, trapping it fast in the so-hot embrace of my so-wet cunt. No, it isn't my wishes, my dreams about them, the clients—but a fact, hard and true, that pushes me harder, faster, upward toward the gleaming peak of a shattering come.

I don't know what they do, you see, but I do know one thing: they enter the Maison Mirage, and with the paying of the fee, and the flipping of some invisible switch, I am theirs— totally, absolutely, theirs.

No fantasy can compete with that fact. No matter who I might be. That's what pushes me over the edge, makes me come and scream with wonderful release: no matter who I am, I am theirs.

INTERCORE

It was the Fall of 2010, and my world wasn't safe: too much out there to catch—or catch you. The forces of law and order were coming down hard, blaming us for a world passing them by.

That, and there were always the new strains.

Only my dead or missing friends had names.

The handle's cybersez.

❈

The sender was a flaming hot number in the cybersea, a dominatrix icon that played games with the boys' heads, and played them ultimately well, and safe. She'd earned, not taken her ID: bytebitch. She wasn't a girlie milking her tits for all the drooling boys. She was a hard dealer—no-nonsense and straight. They didn't like that, expecting sugar and spice, not razors and sure, clear percentages. They'd stuck her with her license plate and she'd kept it, honesty the best policy.

Straight player to another, she invited me into her parlor, stripped that hot icon down to something molten and perverse. We exchanged digitized images of our faces. She had a bowl-cut of darkshade hair, liquid brown eyes, plush lips and cheeks to cut and die on—a mix and match from somewhere Asian and someplace African.

Then that message in alt.sex.freak: *location* (here), *time* (now), and *the deal* (—was this). *Oh, and bring your Toshika.*

And there I was: Not really a street, an alley. The sun eased itself onto jagged skyline teeth; the impalement a pollution-red sunset. Cool shade, the perfume of urban life (piss and wine), the corpses of cars picked clean for their valuable meat and metal. Pools of water and oil, not mixing on cracked streets. Saw no one, but that didn't mean anything—kept my hand in my pocket, wrapped around the cool mean of my little Zilk automatic.

InSane Frisco, Ringold Alley, South of Market—didn't have to live in the city long to know the association: I stood before the gates to Stud Paradise, a graveyard full of memories of gloriously gay alley sex. I found the spot, lit an over-the-counter joint, and waited. The amplified THC mellowed the scene, and for a while I lost the stench and took it all in as a painting: *Portrait of the End of the City*. I waited, appreciating my drug work of art so much I almost missed her.

She walked with purpose down Ringold. Black plastic raincoat, cheap leather boots, a threadbare purple Zo/courier bag—showing what her last straight job was— and coal mine shades. Invisible in the SOMA turf, she was average enough not to catch a second glance.

But I knew her—we'd fucked. But never in the flesh. Cybersea fucking: interactive chat and visuals. Breasts just the right size for filling hands, she said. An electric cunt tight enough to rip condoms off, she said. We'd fucked so many times, but I'd never seen her in the flesh, and I'd never asked for her real name.

Trust.

Bytebitch saw me. Didn't smile. The brown eyes behind the shades might have, but I had no way of knowing. On the corner with me was the picked-clean corpse of a Saab. She moved to the pitted fender and propped herself against it. Cybersez: *Get comfy*. Dropping her bag onto the grimy alley muck, she pulled a cig out of one of her plastic pockets, lit up with the finger-thick flame from a self-defense Hotpoint lighter, and took a long drag of amplified tobacco. Then a quick flick into a puddle of mostly oil, and it came to a hiss-

ing end. My joint followed, and as she pushed off the fender,
I got out my camera—

—my beautiful Japanese Toshika, direct-disc job. Small
and light, straight to read/write CD. In my other hand was
that little German automatic, with its clip of detonator-nylon
rounds: in case of trouble. No extra hand for my dick.

Her SOMA-standard black-latex-gloved hands were on either
side of her SOMA-standard black plastic coat. She arched and
tugged—the first three snaps letting loose, showing in a flash
her valley of pale tit, the start of those "hand-filling breasts."
Hint of something firm and black holding them up. She
posed, leaning back against the Saab's one intact headlight,
running black-gloved fingers over the slope, eyes hidden and
safe behind those black shades, as I let my little Toshika focus
itself, and started to tape.

The bra was black cloth, simple with no stays. One black-
gloved hand scooped down into the right cup, came up with a
white mound of tit—red dot of nipple at the tip. She let it fall
outside the bra. Red nipple, wrinkled and angry, pointed at me
and my lens. I focused as she gripped it between black fingers
and twisted, pulled. Those glasses still on, she hissed and arched
backwards, glass headlight pressing into her ass—the one that
she'd said was "strong enough to crack balls and walnuts."

I taped.

More abuse to that tit—pulling and twisting, holding it
straight out from that gleaming black plastic coat by a nipple.
In my fine Japanese sight, black-lacquered fingernails flashed,
showing what was under the glove (and it flopped to the
ground, dead bird) and traced the sculpture of that tit. A
pinch of soft skin, another hiss.

Still taping. Zoom out—

The pair were out to play. Twin mounds of soft white skin,
rosy pinpoints out and up, erect. She leaned against the auto-
corpse, both tits out to the cooling night air, held up by the

useless bra. Black-lacquered nails dipped into a plastic pocket, dug around and came up with nasty surprises. The first clothespin, intimate pink plastic against pale skin, just above her left nipple. The next followed, part of the pattern, cheap blue plastic one. Slowly, she clipped each plastic clip after the previous, working her way around her tit.

A circle of plastic, hard-toothed clamps ringed that one tit. A flower with the hard button of a tough nipple in the center. Hand a little unsteady, black one this time—special color for a special, special place. When she let go, and it sank its plastic mouth down HARD! onto this already hard button, the hiss that worked its way between her perfect teeth turned from moan to scream in the urban asshole of Ringold alley.

Left followed right: a black-nailed hand dipped into a pocket and paraded another line of clamps. Soon two flowers stared at my fine lens, two flowers of plastic clamps around perfectly conical tits. The one for the center of the left was SOMA-standard black, too. As it bit down, echoing the right, her scream echoed off and through the postindustrial waste-land. As I focused and watched that last one go on, night threw itself down on us. The streetlight hummed, and winked on.

Nailed by hard light, bytebitch staggered back against the pain of her self-imposed torture. Panting, she gripped one side then the other of the plastic raincoat—

Snap, snap, snap, snap.

No underwear. Bare crease, cleft of a smooth, polished cunt. No stubble—industrial shaving for her. She was wet, and she shone and gleamed in the streetlight's hard arc stare. Her cleft was a reflective streak between a plush, valentine mons. She leaned back on the fender and rubbed a palm against her cunt, pressing hard and up, touching palm to clit. A rough, ham-handed masturbation. One foot anchored and she hoisted herself up onto the remains of the headlight mount. Braced, she spread her legs, one against the greasy guts of the brake assembly. Legs spread, she cupped her cunt with one black-nailed hand.

I taped. I taped. I taped. Black like a beetle's back, those polished fingernails went around the red bead of a hard, hard, clit, then up inside the bitch's cunt. Back and forth, back and forth, a liquid action, repetitive and slow. I taped and taped as her hand got wetter and wetter.

Beautiful shot: her hand, her wrist, her arms reflecting the shine of the streetlight, wet from her juice.

Bytebitch hopped off, turned, and I caught it all. She whipped around, the black raincoat flying, wrapping itself around her. Her ass walked backwards, toward me. Her legs, pale and white—boots scuffed, looking like little black cats playing in the junk. She moaned, like a deep-throated kitten getting a barbed dick. The raincoat flipped up and over her.

Bare and perfect, her ass was full and round, and with her legs spread, everything was there for the cold night and the colder lens of my camera: twin cheeks curving up and down and around to a pair of plush wet cunt lips. The glow was real and wet under the hard lights, her lips were parted, churning with her rough jerking off. Three? Four? Was her hand in there? Fisting herself in the harsh light? I saw and taped her lips squirm and bubble with pussy juice. Her moans became hard and quick, forced and stubborn. She grunted while jerking off, deep, masculine sounds. I thought her cunt was going to swallow her, black lacquer and all.

I focused and watched. Focused and watched, precise crosshairs on a wide, wet cunt, foamed and slick from her juice. Thighs shimmering, clit—a perfect shot—a red marble when she pulled back her pointed collection of wet fingertips. I taped, numbers flowing; light levels a rocking bar graph; flickering, fluttering digital time.

Taping, taking—

Her moans changed, like changing shots. I noticed it, the

way you suddenly realize how dark it's gotten. BLINK, BLINK, night. BLINK, BLINK, her moans were restrained, corked.

An acrobatic flip. Flashes of white and other colors from the mother-loving clothespins still on her nipples and tits. I caught, perfectly trapped, her mouth stuffed with plastic cock. Saliva ran down her chin and added gleam to her cleavage. Then slowly, she drew inches and inches of fat plastic sword from her mouth, its head slipping past her lips trailing threads of spit.

It went between her legs. All the marvelous details: one leg went up, one hand fished between her wet thighs for the lips of her wet pussy. As she spread her lips, the other hand snaked the wet dildo in.

Inch, inch, inch—it went up her, her original moans and cries back again with full rutting volume. Bytebitch bent for the camera, leaning back, away from me, eyes still unreadable behind dark shades, mouth open and panting as she swallowed the plastic dick with her cunt mouth.

One hand stayed between her legs—details lost behind the black coat, you could see in the final footage after tweaking and re-enhancement what she was doing—rubbing and stroking, and pulling on that red marble between her wet cunt lips for all she was worth. The other hand was fucking herself with the dildo. Sitting in dark safety later, with my cock and drugs, you could hear her—the rutting bitch—and the sound of her self-fucking. (Good sound quality, those Japanese.) A chorus of wet slaps and sucks perfectly muted and transmogrified by the flesh of her cunt and ass.

No soundtrack needed.

As her cumming came, she rolled off the Saab (and I tracked and followed, taping) and crouched down, squatting above the Ringold filth, all there for the me, for the camera. Shielded eyes up and pleading to the audience, she parted the cloak to show it, show her impalement on her plastic pal, in all its magnificence. Ah, the details: dark cherry clit, like a wet blister between her slick lips. Black plastic cock in and out, in and out, still driven by her other hand.

Perfectly timed with her shuddering moan, it flopped out of her cunt like a beached fish. It slapped onto the dirty asphalt and rolled into the gutter, picking up dirt, grit and that sparkling sand made from ground-down bottles and broken windshields. She came again, moaning deep and frantically batting away the clothespins—snapping them off like hungry, stinging flies she'd suddenly realized were all over her. When the ones on her nipples finally let go, they went zinging into the chain-link fence and clinking against the dead Saab.

Exhausted, deflated, bytebitch collapsed, sliding down onto her own black raincoat, legs kicking out from under her. She sat there for some time, panting, tits going up and down, up and down, beads of sweat raining from softening nipples.

Got it all.

When she had recovered enough, when she no longer saw lights in front of her eyes; when she was together enough to stand, button her coat, grab her bag, pick up her gloves, and adjust her hair and shades, she started off down the severely-lit street. I waited to make sure none of the shadows followed her.

Then I checked my Toshika, watched it all in the tiny viewfinder. All there. Every last bit, bit.

Late tonight, in code, disguised as trivia, as something hopefully below examination, it would go sailing out onto the Sea—profits being split between the star and the crew. She trusted me to do a fair deal.

There's the bottom line: trust. She needed someone to hold the camera, put it together, and do nothing else. She was trusting me to do it—and share the profits—from the only game left in town.

TECHNOPHILE

I almost lost my virginity at fifteen, but his batteries ran low.

He'd shown me the unit, unzipped tight jeans and flashed out the Long Thrust. State, top-of-the-line, implant augmentation. He'd had himself castrated for the best science had to offer. I wanted it the instant I saw it, the burnished, gleam of it. I wanted it bad. Now. Hard. Fast.

My squat was old-wired 220 so its juice-pack couldn't take the flow. In playback, wet-memory, I see him—planes of his face dead in the cheap fluorescents, as he hunts in his bag for the adapter he didn't bring.

In the end, we lit expensive candles and he put his mouth on my cock instead.

His mouth was shockingly wet, not like my dry hand or the spit sometimes to make it easier. It was too slippery, and too hot. I was blazing with shame and self-pity, eyes fake closed and instead watching his head dip down. First a quick spray of over-the-counter anti-viral fog, then it was a wet test embrace on my cock, gentle kisses, then a wet socket over my cock.

Brent, friend of my dealer. I'd been taking longer to slip the black market yen and take the tiny plastic bags, just to watch him stand and pose: first time spotting him was like that first time there in my squat. Thick leathers hiding old cop impact vest, skin-jeans slit to show off log legs, too-tight tee (YANKEE IMPERIALIST VICTIM painted on a stonemason chest), face cragged and street-scarred but with museum planes. Eyes then on the street as they were in my recall of the squat—hidden and refrigerator cool behind convex mirrors of mandatory shades. He may have been handsome, might have made girls wet, boys hard—but I'd heard, and then he'd heard that I'd heard and there in that alley he unzipped and flipped it out. Fuck, I wanted it in me right there.

I was smiling when he lifted up from my hardening cock. Smiling back at his smiling face, at my smiling face reflected in his shades. We smiled at each other reflected over and over as he gently stroked my cock, kissing it, and sucking a mouth-ful of the ridged head (Momma thought cutting sanitary).

The squat was cold and my futon too fucking hard on my back. My jeans were bunched around my legs and my back was crooked funny against my pack. So I put my hand on his head and pushed myself down. So mature for that first time, so controlled from the burning pity and disappointment of that unit, dead and powerless between his legs.

Sloped down onto the futon, I let him suck my cock. The kisses got harder, his tongue began to play with the tip, that little hot hold in the end that sometimes felt like prickles and sometimes like warm steel. I was hard from his mouth there, from his hand gently holding and stroking, from his breath stirring the cool skin from my shaved balls and belly. I was deep inside, eyes really closed, letting his hands and mouth work me up and higher and harder.

My balls began to swell and heat. Something in me wanted, and I let myself put a hand on the crotch of his hot jeans. He closed his thighs on my fingers, trapping them in a denim vice as he made negative moans around my hard cock.

I let him suck more, letting myself burn deep and pissed and disappointed. I felt his teeth slide every inch across the skin of my shaft. I couldn't decide if it was on purpose or acci-dent. And when I thought about it, anticipating or trying to block the hardness of his teeth, it just added something to it. I was harder and harder.

I wanted something again, I couldn't have what I really

wanted but this would do—and from the heat of him on my cock I pushed a sweet little virginal *please* out. I opened my eyes and saw that I had slid myself down to his jeans. I could smell it, that sweet sting-smell of brand-new plastic and his sweat through the thin denim of his jeans. No negative this time. No refusal for the poor virgin boy. The sucking never stopped, the teeth no longer glided (so I guessed he must be pretty fucking good at this), but the hands came out and slipped the jeans down.

Made in the best labs in Shadow Tokyo. Fucking pure lines—a curving, shining downward turning tusk of high-impact plastic nested into a shield of gleaming black chrome. I traced the inert row of decorative indicators that ran along the side of the shaft (as he sucked the head of my cock, just the head, stoking me wet and thumping like a metronome against my balls and stomach), feeling their dimples, and wanting them to light. I kissed the dead head of his unit, tasting a lingering of lube from the last time he'd fucked with it (boy, girl, fist, unknown).

He was sucking so hard now—the coolness was gone, and all I could feel was his hot mouth sucking and licking and sometimes (there, there) the hard glide of teeth in his trained mouth. His fist was still pumping, and my stomach ached with the good hurt of a rough jerk off.

The head of the unit was a kind of different plastic, something so close to skin. I could see with half an eye that the head was anatomically correct, lifelike.

I stroked it, wishing so hard that it was juiced up and like-wise. I wanted it so bad. Wanted it in my own mouth, wanted to really taste that old lube down deep in my throat. Didn't know how to do it, natch—but knew I could, I wanted it so bad. Laying there on the hard futon that smelled of years of mildew, I wanted my virgin ass to take this sweet machine. I wanted it. I could feel it—so hard and buzzing softly with all those marvelous features. Closing my eyes, I could feel it, a great background to his sucking of me. Yeah, I felt it, laying there. Could imagine it so perfectly, as I raised my ass up to meet it. I closed my eyes and dreamed it—that first great touch of it against my asshole as I opened for it, swallowed it and felt the spasmic vibrators, the asymmetric rhythms, the neural stims all start to work on the inside of my asshole. I imagined him taking me deep and hard, only letting the Long Thrust (the Extension Delux Model with the Dynamic Action Features, coupled with the hottest Joy Buzzer software) do some of the fucking. My ass, I thought, would go all jelly, my cock would be, and was, steel. I could feel him slide it into me and out and in and something powerful would start in my ass and it would travel up my spine and out through my cock via my brain—just like they said in their ads on the net—

Fuck, fuck, fuck...I wanted it in my ass and I wanted it in my mouth—but the shaft stayed down, the head stayed slightly cold—like a hot dog from a broken vending machine.

Too late for the reality—I was lost in my fondling, his sucking, the beautiful cockness of the Long Thrust. I felt myself start, felt the rocket start to climb from balls to tip. I could feel the come start to shake and close my eyes. But I kept them open and stared: a Long Thrust Delux there, in the crotch of his hairy thighs. This was one—right in front of me. This was one.

Come jetted from the head of my cock, into his sprayed, disinfected mouth. The come was as hard and hurt as much as my fucking cock. My legs danced. He put his hand on my cold chest as he pumped, sucked and jumped his fist along my shaft. I coated his mouth with my stickiness.

I came all wet and sticky, and all I could think of was Long Thrust between his legs—dead, cold and inert.

SKIN-EFFECT

The city, that night, reminded him of the war.

The yellow sodium lights that receded down the boulevard were like tracers, frozen in a second's fear against the night. The sad woman waiting for her electric bus became a meat whore—one of the camp followers who were always in the towns, the villages, the cities. They offered treats to the meat members of the company but no one ever took them up on it. The fee of a finger, foot, or leg just wasn't worth a fleshly fuck.

A truck rumbling down a street wet with the light rain was really a heavy cruiser looking for somewhere to park and dump its load of ammo, men, or supplies. The light rain was a biodispersal fog. He held his breath walking down the street. Commercial airlines thundering into high orbit were droppers bringing in fresh troops or Free Brazil carriers looking for enough heat signatures to make a smartbomb run worthwhile. A screaming child was a sneaker bullet homing in. A distorted holographic sales pitch was a particle gun cooling down.

It was the war. That night, all of the city was a battlefield.

It was beautiful.

Guardino was lucky he'd managed to slip out from under psych's ropes when he'd been rotated back to the States for a system overhaul. It was easy to slip through when thousands of grunts like himself were going back to get upgraded and have their memories of the last five years dumped—before being sent back out once again for another five years of war.

Guardino was lucky because he liked his memories just fine. He liked hearing Brazie strikes coming in across his dreams. He liked remembering how a heavy lash plasma discharge tube felt.

He liked remembering the screams.

At first he had only liked remembering certain screams, those of the guerrillas and the Brazie soldiers in their deep green uniforms or the other casualties who weren't on his side of the fence. Those screams meant they had won this hill or that town, that village or that valley. Those cries and smells and pools of sticky blood meant rest and rations. But after a surprisingly short amount of time all the sounds, buddies as well as targets, rolled together into the sound of the war.

Around him was the war, or at least a kind of war. People still fought and killed and died in San Francisco, 2129—but for other reasons. The things people were fighting for seemed about as real as a crybaby bomb's auditory hallucinations: food, housing, drugs, even sex. It wasn't real to Guardino, wasn't something that he could relate to. It all seemed more than a little purposeless—unlike the war he had left behind.

Of course, being just a brain supported in a polyarmor combat frame could have had something to do with it.

Still, it was a war nonetheless.

✳

Walking down the wet street, looking for the address he'd been given, Guardino suddenly—and with computer resolution clarity—recalled the medtech's words after Guardino had just lost both legs and most of his lower self to a hummingbird drone: "Sex is all in the mind."

He had been just a baby-faced kid, no more than eighteen. Only one arm gone, replaced by a polished surgical appendage. Prone on a surgical drone's service pad, Guardino had reflexively looked down at the tech's waist and feet—a slight paunch and pink toes—and shrugged him off.

Later, after he'd gotten used to his new lower half—first a

Centipede Mobile and then a Land Strider 2000—and being linked, he'd realized that the kid was right. His cock and balls might be fertilizing some tree somewhere in the Amazon (along with the rest of his lower anatomy) but he'd still get a raging mental hard-on when he charged with the rest of the guys or thought about the times he'd had in some of the villages on R & R. Nothing happened, of course, but he still had a raging: he could feel it like a kind of ghost cock, tingling and throbbing. Sometimes, when the depressants had kicked in after a really good charge, it came close to driving him off the deep end. His cock was gone but fuck, he wanted to fuck...anything.

The only thing he could do in those situations was either damp himself with enough cortical amps to fry the sexual links in his brain or try and scrounge up some combat bitch to link with him. Most of the time when his ghostly cock came back full force and screaming hard, he could find a foxhole cunt and they could get each other off with a link—but then the Army'd started drafting geeks out of the prison system (those with the highest degree of psychotic breaks getting first shot) and he'd stopped hitting up his cooze buddies out of basic survival.

2122 Folsom. The house was a plain Jane alongside its Victorian sisters: badly in need of paint, rolls and coils of fiber-optic cable strewn all over the outside. The only light came from a yellowed biobulb over the front step. The address was right. It was the place.

The steps creaked in complaint as he hauled his combat frame up to the front door. Absently, he caught the tiny ultra-sonic whistle of one of the actuators in his right thigh that meant the smartwire muscle was probably on its last legs. And there: a slight stutter in his waist action (bearings going). Still, he was far from needing a new body. He was still a Gruber MX-1 Armature Combat Frame with a Genetec biosta-tis support cradle. A killing machine with only a few creaks and groans: not bad for five years of slaughter and death.

No doorbell, but he was known, anyway: "Who sent you?" came over a tight band radio transmission. Guardino looked quickly side to side (noticing a slight hesitation in his optical pickups and a faint blur in the infrareds) for the source, but all he saw was peeling paint and warped wood.

He blipped back on the same channel, low power to avoid spillover: "Guy in my outfit. Mitch."

"I know Mitch. Do you know Mitch?" the voice was completely synth—nothing given away in tone or inflection.

"Well enough."

"Well enough to know what he did here?"

"Yes," Guardino sent back. It must have been the right answer: with the thub of heavy steel magnetic bolts the front door swung inwards.

The hall beyond was lit with slight infrared sources. To meat, if would have been completely dark, but to Guardino it was bright as daylight. He stepped inside and the door swung shut behind him. Checking his stern array, he saw that it was really a single sheet of combat grade durasteel.

"Upstairs." Same voice, same amount of information about the sender: zilch.

Guardino was about to mention that the stairs would never be able to support his close to six hundred pounds of actuators and armor, but then he remembered the door, with even the stamp of the Military Inspector System on it, and walked right up. The stairs didn't even complain.

Another door glided smoothly open. Small room, lit as the hallway was with low temp heat sources. In the room—

—Guardino almost left, almost turned and walked down and out. This was what Mitch had whispered reverently about?

"See something you don't like?" the voice said, this time without the filter.

The city wasn't a real war. It was like a kid's toy. Guardino remembered suddenly—again with computer clarity—Little Green Army Men. The city was like those old toys: something powerful and real turned into something safe and playful. He didn't really know what to expect of San Francisco after Mesa Verde, Veracruz, Mount Taco, and Guadalajara—maybe something as real as Brazie soldiers leaping three hundred feet into the air to fall onto you like meteors, preceded and followed by a thunderstorm of tiny anti-personnel missiles that homed in on the tiniest source of heat, the softest noise.

"See something you don't like, mister?" The voice now was soft and weak, so much like, too much like, the meat whores and the hustlers who followed the war like starving dogs. It was too sweet, too empty of anything real—except for the color of your money.

"Nothing I fucking want," Guardino said, letting the good anger come up from inside him, feeling the illegal combat drugs kick in. *It's all just a fucking waste,* he thought, turning slowly. *This is what I fight for? Fucking junk pile—I don't want to fuck it, I just want to fucking kill it.* "Should just fucking kill you."

"You're not the first," she said from the corner, uncoiling herself from the polished hardwood floor. Dragging two of her nonfunctioning limbs, she staggered up on mismatched legs and cocked an intermittent eye at Guardino.

"You don't have what I fucking want."

"But killing me would at least cheer you up, right?" The tight band made a sound close to human female laughter—but only close. Guardino couldn't tell if it was intentional or another malfunction. "Lots of folks out there think the same. The local Wilders last night, in fact. Never was all that much to look at, but they just enhanced the image a bit with a spot welder and a slam hammer."

"Should have finished the fucking job," Guardino said, sick of the pathetic city, the meat on the streets, the clean air, the shocked and scared looks on their faces when they tagged him for what he was: used to death and killing. *Fuck them,* he thought, *fuck them all.* R & R was supposed to be what you wanted, right? Well, fuck, what he wanted right now was more of the same, what he was fucking used to, liked.

Death and destruction.

Yeah, he thought suddenly—clearly—realizing that was just what he wanted and needed for a good dose of R & R. Whistling a little tune he'd heard one of his rock addicted buddies sing just before he'd gotten chopped up by a whacker mine, he said. "So how much to fucking just kill you?"

"Mitch said the same."

"Mitch fucking lost it, man. Don't open your trap about fucking Mitch, all right?"

"Is he dead?"

"Might as well be," Guardino says, stepping in, sizing up the mismatched contraption with a quick sweep of his targeting systems: hairs of brilliant lasers, bursts of micro-millimeter radar, pops of broad-spectrum sound pointed out weak joints, inferior construction, brainbox protected by negligible shielding, unprotected power supply, no visible weapons—none in the room, either. "Mitch got aced, man. Walked where he shouldn't ought to have walked—maybe whistled the wrong fucking tune for all I know. They're putting together whatever they scraped off the fucking palms right now—back in Rio."

"I'm sorry to hear that," the contraption of obsolete parts said with a kind of truly sad whine. "I enjoyed his company."

"Well you ain't gonna enjoy mine," Guardino said, arming his close-in weapons, feeling his core temp rise as the chain-gun whined to firing speed, as the flechette muzzles started to rev up.

Coolly, the mass of hissing and sputtering parts said with a honey-dripping voice: "You've come all this way, up all those stairs, into this room just to kill me? Seems a very simple and quick pleasure."

"You got a better one?" Guardino said, laughing over the carrier-wave between them.

"I have what I offered poor Mitch. If you don't like what I have to offer—" she said as she hauled herself up farther onto a pair of cheap insect legs patched in from an agricultural harvester "—then you can do with me what you will. *Whatever* you will."

"Fucking waste of my fucking time, man," Guardino said, taking the chain-gun and the flechette muzzles off-line, listening to his pinging and chiming frame readjust itself to its new lower temperature.

The claptrap cyborg didn't say anything. She just barely balanced in the corner of the room, hissing and sputtering on her clutch of cheap hydraulics. There was kind of a word between the two of them, hidden somewhere in the carrier wave, or maybe just in Guardino's meat mind, hidden deep in his combat chassis.

Coward?

"What the fuck," Guardino said, stepping up and putting a human-interactive hand on one of her struts. "You ain't gonna hurt me none. Fire me up, fucker. Go ahead and fire me up."

A interface jack coiled serpentine from under her wasp yellow and black power junction array. Guardino sent a snort of disgust: the cable looked barely a 44 gig. A play-toy to someone used to military hardware.

"Remember now," the resident of 2122 Folsom said as the jack hunted out Guardino's input and slithered in, "it's not the socket—it's the *software*."

"My name, by the way, is Pepper—and I'm sure you'll have a *really* good time."

⁂

The transition was faster than Guardino had expected: the "body" rush of the tingling, feverish, switch from his normal sensors and mnemonic pathways was almost instantaneous. One moment he was in the small room in the run-down house in San Francisco, laughing at the assortment of squeaking parts that was "Pepper" and the next...

...grass?

Even the almost invisible background tickling of nutrient fluids around his cortex was absent—something that usually was an anchoring point in whatever simulation or entertainment sim—was gone. In its place was just the soft hint of a slightly warm breeze on a bright summer's day. Grass underfoot, distant rolling hills dotted with the fractal beauty of living trees.

The transition was so sudden, he realized, feeling that breeze, feeling that sun, and looking at those trees, that he didn't even feel his usual military-issue ICE switch on and scan the incoming signals.

Fully trained in combat anti-intrusion systems, Guardino quickly reached up with a mental finger and activated his scanning pull-down. A-Okay. The scan showed nothing but a simple, though highly dense, sim signal. Nothing nasty, nothing alarming.

Trees, sun, a warm breeze.

"Hello," Pepper said, stepping out of the air.

Freckles, a wave of brilliant, burning-red almost black in its blondness. A girl's body—all lean and tight and angular—just on the verge of the rapid decline of age: breasts pale and firm, dotted with bright crimson nipples. Cunt lips barely visible behind a thin red cloud of hair. Naked, she stood on a low hill with Guardino. As casually as he could, Guardino examined himself.

He was himself: before that ambush, before that sunburst cascade, before the horror of Rio Bravo and that surge mine outside of La Paz. He was dark, strong and powerful. He even felt the faint tickling of his mustache under his nose and the soft weight of the thick steel ring in his left nipple. In the warm breeze, naked before the naked Pepper, he felt himself tense and sway gently, the familiar sensations of a meaty cock starting to get good and meaty hard.

"Is this good? Or would you prefer something else?" Pepper said, with a smile.

Piss and blood and concrete. Angry drunks. Bunks. Bars and a stainless steel toilet. He hadn't been there before, but knew it from a thousand jerks, from a thousand comes: A jail cell block from some unknown, unnamed prison from the last century: "screws," "squealers," and "punks." Guardino was "Butch," a badass killer, and Pepper was a visiting nurse trapped in the cell block after a riot. First he'd have her, then he'd share her with the rest of his "punks."

"Please don't, Butch..." whimpered Pepper from the bunk. Guardino was kneeling between her silk-stockinged legs with his iron cock pressing against her asscheeks, getting kissed by a hungry and squirming asshole. "Please, *please*, let me go. I promise I won't tell the guards—"

Guardino's cock was steel, iron, metalloy—it was like a length of angry snake strongly caught in a tiger's leap from his crotch. Part of it was that he was in a limbo simulation, where he wasn't tired, hungover, or even flesh—Guardino was pure mind, and thus, pure fucking lust. Another part of it, of his throbbing cock, was that he was smelling (urine, piss, anger, fear), feeling (the coarse material of the cot, Pepper's starched nurse's skirt hiked over her pale ass), hearing (the pure whimpering of Pepper, the screams and yells of the other prisoners) and ... all of it something that he had only visualized in heated flashes as he jacked off. He was walking, and could be fucking, in a perfect, high-fidelity, realized fantasy.

His cock wasn't just throbbing, it was aching.

"Or this," Pepper said from under him, a hint of mischievous slyness in her voice.

Smoke, booze, and drinks. Recall slammed into Guardino and he knew where he was as certainly as he knew his name: the Deep End, a GI hole in Veracruz. It was a bar, whorehouse, drug den, and second home.

He was meat again and the taste of the End's cheap, watered-down booze was smoldering in his gut. He was sitting in one of the rickety chairs, partially blinded by one of the overhead lights, and in his lap, sticking her tongue down his throat was Kitten, one of the dancers—his favorite whore.

"Miss me?" Kitten said, releasing the kiss and pressing her ridiculously huge, and incredibly lovely, bare tits into his face. "Miss them?" Her voice was just enough of Pepper's to give the illusion away.

Still in his lap, her big-hipped, big-titted weight crushing down on him—but not nearly enough to stop his cock from aching with a painfully determined erection—she pressed her huge, firm, gleaming, sweaty tits against his face. Her nipples, the size and strength of thumbs, grazed his cheeks and ears like fingertip caresses. Somewhere, more powerful than the stink of his own BO and the grass smoke that fogged the club, he could smell her cunt, her fucking-machine desire. Kitten always had this really strong smell—and it was like a hot wire jammed into his brain. One whiff of her pure animal rutting smell and his cock would be hard for hours and he could fuck and fuck for days. Maybe it was some kind of drug, an implant, or even a subsonic leash, but whatever the cause, Guardino never seemed to care. And then, there, with Pepper somewhere calling the shots, he didn't care again.

"How about this?" Pepper said, smiling Kitten's broad-mouthed smile.

Guardino was sixteen. He was standing again in the laundry room of his parents' condo. The smells of childhood smashed into him: hot rubber, steam, bad wiring, soap, and mold. He was sitting on the steel folding table, watching the clothes spin and churn in the machines, absently turning the pages of a Japanese softcore interactive mediabook. Mrs. Boyd was hauling her own clothes out of another machine, bending over and straightening up—giving the young Guardino a magnificent view of her divinely strong ass through her simple skirt.

Back then, he hadn't known what was coming. Now, he did. His cock was as strong as his sixteen-year-old arm. It did more than tent his simple school running pants, it practically reached out past his leg to cop a feel.

"Been running much?" Mrs. Boyd said, standing and turning, all the time her eyes on the pale crown of his cock.

"Some," he said, had said, too shocked to say anything beyond the empty obvious.

Her hand lifted and landed casually on his pants, on his cock. She squeezed it gently, as if to make sure it was real and not a trick of the bad lights. "Want me to suck it?" she said with Pepper's voice.

Guardino had nodded, did nod.

She struggled a bit with his running pants till intelligence rolled back into Guardino's brain and he lifted himself up enough off the hard steel table for her to get them down. His cock sprang up full and screamingly hard, a fat bead of milky pre-come dotting the tip.

Mrs. Boyd, the tight and firm and pouty Mrs. Boyd, about twenty years beyond him, got down on her knees and took his cock in her mouth and started to suck.

God, did she suck. Looking back, and then, right then, as well, Guardino realized that she either must have been a frustrated expert with few to practice her skills on or she had just been starving for a cock in her mouth. Mrs. Boyd was an incredible cocksucker—she licked and sucked and kissed and nibbled till Guardino was just about to scream and fire off down her throat.

Back then, he had, and Mrs. Boyd, shocked by what she'd done, had squealed and screamed in her own shame and run off, come dribbling down her cheeks.

But this wasn't then: she sucked and sucked more and more, till Guardino was bucking his hips up and down off the table, fucking her pale lips.

"Come here and look," she said as she climbed up onto the table next to him and lifted her simple skirt.

Guardino got down off the table and did what he had always wanted to do to Mrs. Boyd. On his knees on the cold, mold-streaked concrete of the laundry room, he pressed his mouth to her furry, steaming cunt and returned the favor.

Mrs. Boyd, shaking her head with involuntary jerks of pleasure, grabbed his sixteen-year-old head and forced his eager and energetic lips all over her cunt: her puffy, silken lips; the strong globes of her ass; the knotted muscles of her thighs and—with a screaming, shuddering orgasm—the twitching bead of her clit.

"Or here?"

"Or this?"

"Or that?"

"Them?"

Tits and cunts and bellies. Hair and faces and eyes. Nipples and thighs and assholes. Cheeks and feet and hands. Farmers' daughters, babysitters, milkmaids, French maids, Nazis, ballerinas, waitresses, nurses, and doctors. Sucking his cock, sitting on his face, rubbing his with their tits, pissing warm on his chest. Fucking them up the ass, fucking their faces, fucking their cunts. Sucking, fucking, stroking, coming, coming, come....

Then he did, an earthquake release that sparked throughout his meat and his circuits—a flashing, painful burst of knee-trembling pleasure that tripped his breakers and almost snapped his safeties. Through and around and between, the burst of pure come rocked, twisted, and would have brought tears to his eyes—if he had eyes.

When he came out the other side it felt like he was a different man.

✳

"I don't believe we've been formally introduced," Pepper said, shifting slightly with an accompanying hiss and spit of misfiring hydraulics.

"My name is Guardino. Lionel Guardino, Mistress."

"My, you are a strong one, aren't you? I'll bet you've got really big muscles and plenty of firepower, too. Even illegal mods, too, am I right?"

Guardino gladly rattled off his capabilities and his entire inventory of weaponry, smiling (electronically) all the while.

"That's very good," Pepper said, stretching out a broken and misfiring mannequin hand to gently stroke his armored chassis, "very, very good. Now we're going to go meet some friends of mine. Well, not really friends, you see; they're Wilders. Bad Wilders. They did some very bad things to your Mistress. Very, very bad. They hit her with a spot welder and a slam hammer."

Guardino made a noise somewhere between a growl and a steam whistle going off. "I'll kill them."

"Yes, you will, won't you? You'll kill them nice and—well, nice and really *messy*."

Guardino opened his ports, let Pepper jack herself into his support software, then picked her up and gently, very gently, secured her leaking, misfiring frame to his own hardpoints.

After a few minutes, when they were down the stairs and out the door, he sent a very soft, weak message to her: "Mistress?"

"Yes, Guardino?"

"If I kill these very bad Wilders for you could we, I mean,

if you'd let me, I mean—"

"Make love again?"

Abashed and humiliated: "Yes, Mistress."

"We'll see, Guardino, we'll see: if you do a very good job of killing them. We'll see."

SIGHT

"A superb item," the Elgin said. Cortez's father, when he saw the Elgin for the first time, called them poor sketches of a lowly specimen. Now it was all Cortez could see when he looked at them. "Lovely of ... line. Much desire for personal ownership." Gray hands on cool metal, following the curvature he'd spent hours achieving. "Yes, affirmative; lovely of line."

"Naturally," Cortez said as McGuiness, beaming his money changer's dentistry, tapped out the details of the exchange on his computerized desktop. "For the Citizens of the Elgin I only do my greatest."

The Elgin tapped the side of its head, gray fingers on gray cheek. In their natural habitat they didn't have faces, per se. The immobile masks they wore on Earth were a polite gesture, as was the tapping to indicate pleasure. "No one can accomplish what you accomplish," it said, in a hollow, synthesized voice. "No one brings into life such...beauty."

"Of course," Cortez said, sipping from a flute of excellent champagne and smiling. Faces or none, almost a decade of dealing with them had brought him a kind of artistic appreciation of their twisted, leaden forms; a way of seeing what he knew others couldn't see. He could even read their emotions, after a fashion: the posture of impatience, the tension of humor, the rippling of their heavy skins that indicated insult. Some were a puzzle, still—like the gleaming in the eyes of the one looking at his works—but he knew, given time, he'd manage to decipher it as well. After all, he thought, continuing to smile as the Elgin bent to speak its language into McGuiness's

computer and seal the deal, was he not Jesus Cortez? Many
had tried, all of them had failed: only the works of Cortez
were of interest to the Elgin. They came, they saw, they nodded politely, but it was only his work that they bought and
took home. No Rembrandt, no Monet, no Calder, no Leonardo,
no Michelangelo. Only Cortez.

"Two liters, uncoded nano; fifteen of monomolecular suspension gel; one of diametric genetic material," McGuiness
said with a wry smile, his fingers tapping at the pulsing, dancing images between himself and the Elgin.

"For such...beauty," the Elgin intoned, managing to bring
awe to his synthetic voice, "I cannot do but agree."

"Was there any doubt?" Cortez said, raising his vintage in
salute to himself.

✳

A real estate magazine had called the cost of his villa 'obscene'.
Reading it, Cortez had smiled, looking down on the little
writer of the article from his lofty villa. For an artist, there
could be no price on perfect lighting.

Mariposa had that, in delightful abundance. In the morn-
ings, the sun rose above distant, saw-toothed mountains,
lending a perfect dawn glow. At midday, it would be idyllically
overhead, casting sharp-edged shadows on his marble
veranda; and at dusk it would sink with bloody warmth into
a liquid-steel sea. For that, he could never pay enough.

It also had other qualities almost as attractive. It was
remote, only his personal maglev line between home and the
nearest city tubeway. And it was high on a cranium-ridged
outcropping of rock, so he could look out on the desolate
beauty of the plains—a bleak geologic canvas that didn't dis-
tract his perfect artist's eye with unnecessary trees, or other
natural clichés.

When he was in the city he was forced to mix with all

sorts of humanity and non-humans such as the Elgin who seemed to consider contact with him a status thing. Often he'd wryly debated the possible supplementary income of selling locks of his hair to the lead-colored visitors. But at Mariposa he reveled in isolation. Prosman, his valet; Guin, his chef; and Conners, his security man, were all who were regularly allowed up the hill from the maglevline. Even McGuiness kept his visits short and business-like, knowing how irritable Cortez could be with intrusions.

"This way, Miss," Conners said, indicating the free-flowing staircase crawling up the steep outcropping of rock. Rosalinda Valier, twenty-five, student at the New York Academy of the Arts. Painter. One arrest, three years previously, at a demonstration against the proposed quarantining of Elgin dignitaries. An interview with the elusive, world-renowned artist, inexplicably granted. "Watch your step, Miss," Conners said, a sly smile working across his thin lips.

"Th-thank you," the girl said, accepting the big Englishman's huge hand. Her nervousness manifested itself vocally with a hesitant stammer and physically as cool, clammy hands.

"No problem, Miss. That's what I'm here for," Conners said, a quick wave of anger at her innocence making him avert his eyes. "This way," he said, gesturing up the stairs. "He's expecting you."

⁂

Cortez paid no attention to what she said, instead looking at the shape of her body under the white blouse, black skirt combo she wore. In her dossier on his nightstand display screen, she seemed much younger—a fact that made him lose even more interest in what she was saying. Finally, when he realized that she'd stopped speaking, he said, automatically: "I feel a responsibility to share my insights with the world, but not to line the pockets of the global information culture. I much prefer to speak directly to the people, rather than to the companies who only care for the pesos my messages will bring them."

"I understand completely," she said. "In fact, I was going to use that as a focus of my article; how despite your important role in relations with the Elgin you still take time to share your thoughts with the rest of us."

"Yes, yes; you're very perceptive. It would be too easy to play among the rich, or to only create for governments hungry for the technology our visitors trade for my humble works. I much prefer to give to the people of this world, to show everyone that Jesus Cortez is just a man at heart."

She smiled, and he found himself once again hours ahead, feeling the play of those delightful cheekbones under his fingers, tasting the salt of her lips. He wondered, letting his mind race, about the feel of her skin, the size and texture of her nipples, the softness between her strong thighs. He promised himself a touch of her bare arm as soon as possible—not a good test, he knew, but contact enough to sate himself till he could expose more of her to Mariposa's glorious light.

"Come, come—let me show you my studio. It is a place I rarely show anyone. But you, I sense, would truly appreciate it. Come—"

If that materialistic writer would have shaken his intelligent head at the cost of the villa then he surely would have felt a pain in his chest at the cost of Cortez's studio. It was not information he released, but the roof of his studio was the largest single piece of crystal glass in the world. Perfectly round, perfectly domed, it had been crafted by the Elgin in payment for a special job. He didn't know all their emotional states yet, but when he'd unveiled that particular work the dance of their hinged primary and secondary hands could only have been called ecstasy—an ecstasy that brought him his optically perfect ceiling.

She stood, shocked silent by the golden afternoon light flooding through the roof. Along the walls, a museum of tools. In the center, a dais supporting a half-finished work.

He talked, filling the vast space with his fluid tones, his singsong accent. "You are an artist too, so you'll know why I must have light. Without light there is nothing. So here I bring in the best of all possible light. I bring it here to use in my work. I allow nothing but beauty to enter here, nothing but the best. I cannot work with anything else. Here, you see this? The finest of tools, imported from Japan, made by a master. Here, too, this silver I have especially smelted, carefully forged. Incredibly pure. Here, this wire is pure platinum. Nothing but purity, nothing but beauty; after all, how can one make beauty without beauty to start with, eh?"

She said something in response, something intended to be a passionate agreement; he only heard the tones, listening for the dance of inflections, the meaning behind the publicity she was shoveling out. "—this," the meaning slipping through as she walked towards the work in progress, "is beautiful."

"Gracias," he said, walking up to it, running his thick-fingered hands along the cool metal of the sculpture. "I am fashioning it for the Elgin ambassador. He has two of my pieces already, but he wants something special. Very precise he was, dimensions, materials, and the like. For him, of course I will do anything. But it still needs...well, how can one judge what a work needs, eh? Sometimes it yells, sometimes it barely gives a whisper. We can do nothing but listen. This one...this one is all but silent. Its voice is low indeed." He paused for dramatic affect, letting his touch linger on the cool metal for a long minute. "Hush, let me listen," he added at the end of the stretched time, even though she'd been silent the whole time. "Ah, ah, yes!" he proclaimed, dancing away from the sculpture. "Yes, I hear it now! This one needs a mother to help give it birth, a mother to help it into this world. It cries out—can you not hear it—for one of incredible beauty to show it the way into this, our world."

He took hold of her shoulders, moved her next to the work so he could see both on the dais. "Yes, yes, stand here." He darted from her to the unfinished work, his eyes seemingly pulling form and lines from the sculpture to her, from her to the sculpture. A frown slipped over his lips, pulling his whole body down. "No, no, this is not right. No, this isn't working." He plucked at her blouse. "Off, off with it all. There can be no interference."

She started; his callused fingers were surprisingly nimble with her buttons. He hoped she wouldn't scream, wouldn't pull away. He knew he was clumsy. Compared to steel, silver, gold, and iridium, women crumbled in his hands, turning to sadness and disappointment. When they did push his hands away, when women looked in his eyes, he knew they didn't see the shimmering artist. He knew they saw little Jesus with the acne scars and the little dick. But he was lucky, or his money and fame were a wonderful lubricant. Most of the time, he didn't care; in fact, the only time he did care was when he was poised, fingers at buttons, thumb hooked in the elastic of a pair of panties.

Rosalinda Valier, twenty-five, student at the New York Academy of the Arts, painter, didn't scream, cry or pull away. Hesitated, yes, hands on his, his on the buttons of her blouse, but she didn't take them away. She shook, quietly, a little frightened, a little excited, very confused.

"Here, here," he said, the delight he felt at unwrapping a special gift apparent in his voice. The buttons fell away, her hands dropping slowly to her sides.

Skin, marvelous skin. Next to the fires of reflection on the unfinished work she was glowing marble. Her skin had a quality, a deep buttery color, that made him pause with a slow, whistling intake of breath. Slim shoulders, petite arms, delicate wrists and hands. Not the hands of an artist, he sarcastically thought. Without asking, she brought her hands to the straps of her lacy white bra.

"Yes, yes, yes," Cortez said, distantly aware that he was speaking. The bra slipped forward, suspended on the fullness of her breasts for a delightful moment. Watching, eyes drinking in every detail, Cortez wished that moment would last forever, the suspension of firm young skin, the knowledge that in a beat of his hammering heart he would see the miracle of her body. Suspense or the knowledge of his glorious accomplishment in acquiring the sight of her, naked, he couldn't say—but his excitement stood like one of his finely honed steel tools in his canvas pants.

Her breasts were more than beautiful. Cortez held his breath as she stood revealing herself to him. Big, but not gross, with a sweet upturn, gently flowing from the pure alabaster skin of her chest to the brown roughness of hardening nipples. Just seeing them, Cortez felt a kind of artistic bliss flash down through his body. He was half enraptured, half dumbstruck, all aroused.

She smiled shyly, as if suddenly aware of standing half-naked in the vast, illuminated space—but, the real shock came with her growing awareness of the excitement flashing between them. Slowly, she started to bring her hands up to the delicious swell and gentle upturn of her breasts.

Cortez stepped forward in two quick strides, embracing her. Rosalinda quickly sighed, a deep release of tension that twisted his heavy locks in its breeze as he bent his mouth to her neck. He was lost in a second, lips to her sweet skin, hands to the beauty of her breasts. Her nipples crinkled more and more, growing beneath his quick touches.

Firmly, hands pressing into the silken skin of her bare shoulders, he turned her around so that her lean back neatly fit the shape of the sculpture. His mouth slipped from the tender slope of her neck to her lips. Surprisingly hot; he felt himself scalded by the tenderness of her mouth, the strength of her tongue. He thought he would burst into flame, blasted into composites by the heat radiating off the girl. Pausing, retreating, he broke the kiss with a single step back. A mistake, for he could look on her afresh. Delightful descent of shoulders, full breasts of a divine architecture, nipples wrinkled up full and hard, gentle rise of belly, a dimple of a navel. Looking at her, he felt his heart hammer quick, his cock strain painfully in his pants, his eyes dart all over her beauty, his breath catch in his chest.

Then he looked beyond her, as if his eyes couldn't take the sight of her anymore, to rest on the half-finished sculpture— its curving reflections and mirror shapes.

He stared. He started, and then he stared some more. He didn't want to see, but against his will he did: in its shimmering lines, in its polished surface, he saw what he hadn't seen before. The Elgin didn't have faces, it was true, but they had expressions, and he knew them all. All but one. Until that day, in his studio with the young girl. Until that day he looked beyond her beauty to see the shimmering reflection of his own face.

✳

She hated the stove. It had always annoyed her, annoyance rising to fury when it refused to work, or worse worked only part of the time, turning cakes and lasagna into half-frozen disasters. But now she really hated it because it would have been so easy to fix. One call. Just one call to any one of the new services that'd been hounding her since she came back from Mariposa and the stove would be fixed; she could even have a brand new, spectacular Wolf if she wanted.

Rosalinda slammed the door, absently watching the perpetually dirty elements jump. She could even buy a new, fuzzy-logic microwave. Hell, she could even pay someone to come in and cook for her.

She couldn't blame them really, she just resented the hollow reasons for their pursuits. They really didn't want to know what she thought, what had happened between herself and Cortez. They just wanted to know why the most important artist on the planet wasn't creating anymore. They wanted to know what she'd seen, what had happened, and—when the demands got angry—what she'd done.

When they left her alone long enough she couldn't help thinking about what had happened two months before. Sometimes she was angry that it had been her, of all people, to have been there, then. Sometimes she cried, not really understanding why, but relishing the release.

Other times she just stared at the walls, trying to get back there and understand what had happened.

She didn't know what to expect from the future. The past had been so large, so important that it blotted out any thought of tomorrow. Everything important was back there in Mariposa.

Until her doorbell rang.

＊

"Rosalinda?"

Her first reaction was that he'd shrunk somehow. With that, reasons: starvation, disease (please, no, she thought in a flash of selfishness), and even perspective. He didn't look like the single connection between humanity and Elgin, he just looked like a more than middle-aged Latin man: short, with a slight paunch; graying, curly black hair; mushroom nose; sparkling eyes. He didn't look like Jesus Cortez, and he was too small to leave standing in the hall.

"I..." she started to say, but then simply said, "Please, come in."

"Gracias. Thank you. No one knows I'm here. Conners is quite skilled, but still my employee. I told him to take in a show."

"How did you find me?" she said, trying not to say what she really wanted to: why did you come here?

"Resources. I have more than anyone deserves. No one else knows, Rosalinda. I know how hard this must be for you."

Do you really? she almost said. "Thank you." What she was thanking him for she didn't know. But seeing him standing in her little apartment, her anger faded. He was awfully small. "How are you?" she said, surprised at how much she cared.

"I'm so sorry," he said, looking at her feet. "I have put you in a hard place, Rosalinda. I never meant for this to happen. Things have just—what do they say? 'Knowledge is a dangerous thing'? I have had some dangerous knowledge. No, not your fault. But you helped me see something I didn't want to see."

She instantly wanted to offer him tea, coffee, anything but having to hear any more. She knew knowledge was a dangerous thing; she'd been burned by his proximity before, and she was shy of blisters.

"You are so beautiful," he said, suddenly, looking into her eyes. "I have had others, yes, you must know that, but you...so beautiful."

She wanted to hold him, right then. Just hold his little body, hold him close. It wasn't so much a mothering as a return to what had happened to them in his studio. Sometimes she looked back on it with puzzlement, sometimes with shame, but many times she longed for the heat again. The heat, and that special light.

"I think of you so often, Rosalinda. You are for me...an ideal? I hope I did not soil you."

Without a thought: "No, not at all. Not at all."

"I am glad for that. So glad." He changed the subject so drastically she was dizzy, disoriented. "We know so little about them, you know. Least of all why me, why what I make moves them so. I thought I knew. But, Rosalinda, I didn't. I wanted to think they found my work beautiful, that it moved them in some way." He paused, looked again at the floor. "It did, Rosalinda. It did. Seeing myself reflected as I looked at you...naked, I recognized what they saw in my work. I lusted after you, you excited me. And for them, my work the same." He laughed. "A pornographer for a race. A compliment I guess."

He turned slightly, moving towards the door. "I'm sorry to have used you. I'm sorry to have debased you as I did. I'm sorry for many things, but that is something that has burned me, down deep. I just wanted to say...I'm sorry."

His hand was on the knob and her hand was on his shoulder. He turned, shocked, maybe even frightened that she might be angry. Instead, her lips grazed his. "What?" he said, the word small.

"Stop," she said. "Don't go." He seemed so wounded, so hurt. His Madonna defaced by a stiff cock, his Goddess ruined by a bead of come. "I don't mind—I didn't mind." She laughed, hand still on his shoulder. "I might have had better seductions, but I didn't mind."

He seemed to deflate a bit more, but then smiled as she led him back into the tiny apartment. "It had always worked for me before," he started to say, but the words faded as her lips met his.

They stood and kissed for a long time, working their way slowly through their confusion till their bodies took over. Hers stiffening, moistening; his just stiffening. Her lips were going home, tasting the best things of the past. Plush silk, firm tenderness.

Her hand reached down and felt his hardness, took long minutes exploring its shape and rigidity through his pants. She knew he was blushing, that his shame was red on his face. She wanted to comfort him but she also knew what she wanted—and knew what was best for him.

She dropped to her knees. "I want to suck your cock," she said, thinking, *Take that you fucking Madonna.* Fumblings, everyday underwear, then what she wanted. Big, hard, beaded with a pearl of pre-come, the continuance of what had been interrupted months before.

She licked, she kissed, she stroked with firm fingers, she sucked—yes, she sucked. She took the head of his cock in her mouth and relished its hardness, its salty flavor, its obvious sexual presence. She licked him, sucked him, kissed him until his hands could only rest on the top of her head and the only sounds he could make were a series of deep moans.

No, not yet, she thought as her hands teased him, tangling and untangling the stiff curls around his fat balls. No, not yet. She stood, quick, never taking her stroking hand from his cock. She'd been wearing her ugly, ordinary clothes and was grateful. No fancy stays, buttons, clasps or hooks. Sweat pants, everyday cotton panties. Easy to slip down, easy to kick away.

She bent over the sofa, spreading her long legs. "Fuck me," she said hoarsely, her voice deep in powerful rut. "Come on, Cortez," she said. "Fuck me."

He did. Slowly, timidly, as if frightened of her cunt shattering under overly-vigorous thrusts. But she would have none of that. This wasn't the time for timidity, this was a time for cock in cunt, dick in pussy. She pushed back, devouring his cock. Soon he was thrusting properly, hammering his length in and out of her so-wet, hungry self.

Time lost meaning, suspended. Just her cunt, his cock, mixing in a wet, sliding rhythm. In and out, in and out, for all eternity. But then eternity started to expand. It felt like soaring, like climbing some easy hill. Up and up and up and up until there was nowhere else to go but out. Him into her cunt, she into the stratosphere.

Collapsing, they mixed, legs and arms a jumble, at the

foot of her couch. Before he could sleep, before he could remember anything of what had been haunting him, she said a few words into his ear: "Beauty did that. Lust did that. You do that, to them. Isn't it good?"

⁂

"English words do not suffice, and Elgin words would have no meaning to you," the Elgin said, primary hands frozen, secondaries fluttering like maddened hummingbirds.

"I'm just so glad you liked it. It means a great deal to me," Cortez said, smiling innocently and broadly. Behind him, he knew McGuiness was also smiling—but his grin was not as important, hinging on just the sale.

"It gives me...unimaginable joy. Unimaginable." The Elgin said, its secondaries skating over the smooth surface, an obvious caress.

"Then I am happy I have succeeded," Cortez said, stretching his hand out to wrap it around Rosalinda's waist. "Your pleasure is mine."

THE SHOW

Outside, the city was a night sky of square stars: a galaxy of windows, a constellation of consumers among flashing, pulsing advertisements—product-placement nebulae.

Smoke was standing in one window, a rectangular sun of a different type, looking out at the spectacle of nighttime New York. He felt like he should be sneering, thinking something arrogant—like how he, behind this one window, wasn't just another sun, but rather a media prank nova ready to blast the consumer galaxy of New York with mind-blowing light. Yeah, something like that. Instead, what he was really thinking was how his new boots—nice though they were—were killing his feet, that he only had seventeen dollars and fifteen cents in his checking account...and that he was really worried about Jayne.

"Well, the Master has worked his magic," Truck said from where he was sprawled in a far corner of the tiny Times Square apartment, circuit board in his lap, a faint plume of gray smoke rising from the soldering iron in one hand. "All he needs now is for the talent to do its thing."

Meaning Smoke and Jayne. "Give it a rest, will ya?" Smoke said, still looking out the window at the busy drones of New York.

"Hey, man, just laying it out, that's all. We've only got a day or so before someone notices my expert hacks. We've really got to do this thing and get the hell out before then."

The apartment wasn't even seedy. Beside the one window, it was just a stained sink under a flaking mirror, a tiny pressboard nightstand, a (nonworking) wall sconce shaped like a seashell, and the bed. The mattress felt way too soft, like lying on a decaying marshmallow, and the piss-colored bedspread smelled of ancient cigarettes and mildew.

The atmosphere wasn't why they were there. "I got it, I got it," Smoke said, running a thin hand through his long dark hair. He sighed. "But I can't force her or anything, man."

"Didn't ask you to—just stating the facts, is all. Wouldn't want my beautiful work to go to waste, you know."

Running through the interior wall was a special trunk line—part of the Tyrano-Vision screen overlooking Times Square's control system. The circuit board in Truck's lap was patched skullduggerously into it—linking the tiny solid-state camera duct-taped to the wall directly to the eighty-foot monster screen. Their first act of Awareness Terrorism—as they called it—had been to alter some dozen or so billboards throughout Manhattan, turning cigarette ads to GOT CANCER? After that, they'd placed OUT OF DISORDER stickers on hundreds of vending machines all over the island. It was just Smoke, Truck and Jayne—but they'd made *The Daily News, The Times,* and all kinds of local TV stations. Tonight was going to be their coup de grace: a skillful manipulation of corporate propaganda to bring their message to the milling throngs of Times Square—an artistic assault on the plastic culture imposed at dollar-point on the people of New York: Smoke and Jayne, eighty feet tall, fucking on the Tyrano-Vision screen.

A shave-and-a-haircut knock brought Smoke from the window to the scarred and battered door. Jayne stood in the hall, looking sheepish and small despite her army surplus jacket and black parachute pants,.

There was just one problem—and it wasn't with Truck's hackwork. "I'm going to check the jumpers on the roof again," he said, carefully putting the circuit board aside. "Let me know if you guys get that romantic spark going." He slipped past Jayne and vanished toward the back stairs.

Jayne stepped in, closing the door behind her. "Just call me frigid," she said with a wry smile, slipping off the glasses and dropping them onto the bed.

Smoke put his arms around her. "Fuck that," he said with a smile. "You do what you want to do. If you just don't want to do it, that's cool."

She shook her head. Jayne wasn't a small slip, she was full-bodied and outrageous—or at least normally outrageous. Her face was puckish, her lips and eyes set on Perpetually Amused, and her body language usually broadcasted Fuck with Me If You Dare—but right then she was smaller, drained, and shy and Perpetually Amused seemed more like Sad Self-Deprecation.

Smoke felt something down deep, an ache at seeing the transformation. He liked his wild Jayne, his Jayne who liked to fuck on the L line; who so liked to walk around his scummy little West Side apartment, proudly nude. He liked to hear her mumble when they made out, telling him in explicit detail what she wanted to do, was going to do to him, with him. It was only because of outrageous Jayne that the Times Square prank had even been considered—and she'd seemed all for it. In fact, she seemed more than all for it for weeks until, that is, the day before, when outrageous Jayne, the Jayne who liked to flash her plump tits at passing tour buses, had come down with a severe case of...shyness?

"It's just...I don't know," Jayne said, pushing herself back into Smoke's thin arms. "I'm just nervous, that's all—and it freaks me out."

"Doing it?"—Doing it in front of a thousand strangers— "Or being nervous?"

"Both, I guess," she said, turning carefully around until her lips were just about even with Smoke's. "It's weird—and I don't like it."

Smoke didn't say anything—instead he just bent down

and kissed her. Jayne was wearing her favorite lipstick, Urban Decay, and the familiar heavy slickness of her lips on his made Smoke's breathing start to come fast and quick.

"Whatever turns you on," Smoke said, slowly drawing his lips across hers, "or doesn't is cool with me. Okay, babe?"

"Yeah ..." she said, her voice sad and heavy. She put her face against Smoke's chest. His FUCK THE FUCKERS T-shirt was barely clean but that was good, because Jayne could relax into its comfortable smell, sagging just a bit in his arms. "I know. But I really wanted to, you know? I've been thinking of nothing else for the last few days. Up here," she said, pulling an arm free to tap her forehead, "It really gets me going. The idea of all those people watching us, getting turned on while we do it ... oh, man, but something gets caught down here," she shifted her finger down between her plump breasts, "it gets stuck somehow, gets all mixed up. I don't know what to do."

"You do whatever you want to do, babe. Don't worry about Truck or me—fuck, what's more important? Screwing with the people out there or doing what you want to do? We can fuck with them anytime—it's you that's really important."

"Thanks," she said in a sweet little voice, a little girl's tones from the young woman's full mouth. She kissed him again, from gentle to a slow, hot, dance of firm tongues. "I want to—I'm just scared," she said, breaking the kiss long enough to say it.

"Yeah, I know." Smoke knew he should have been all caring and shit, but his body wasn't listening. A hard cock wasn't really "caring": in his battered, threadbare jeans his dick felt like another arm, one that throbbed towards Jayne. "It would have been fun, wouldn't it?"

"Oh, yeah," Jayne said, running a finger around where his nipples made small tents in his T-shirt. "All those people down there, looking up at us. I'm such a freak—but it really gets me going."

Smoke returned the gesture, opening her jacket and circling her nipples with his fingertips, but Jayne responded more urgently—the tents that appeared on her own T-shirt were five times larger, and much more sensitive. She arched her back against Smoke's methodical circles, and her eyes slightly glazed over. "Me, too," Smoke said.

"I've been thinking about it a lot," Jayne said as Smoke pushed her heavy jacket off her shoulders and it fell to the ugly yellow carpet. "How we'd start by just standing there, up on the screen, just the two of us...naked. Oh—"

The thought, but also Smoke lifting her T-shirt up and placing a single, firm kiss on her left nipple made her voice trail off. But her voice and words returned as he gave the same treatment to her right nipple. "You'd be hard. Oh, yeah, hard like you are now, right? Fucking hard: cock all big and pretty. Bobbing up and down just a bit, maybe even a little bit of pre-come at the tip. Just the way I like it." As she spoke, Jayne rubbed her hand down the front of Smoke's jeans, playing with the fat bulge, tracing the outline of his hard cock. "Just the two of us, eighty feet high, naked...hard and..."

"Wet?" Smoke said, lifting her shirt up and off as it finally passed over her head he leaned forward and kissed her, long and firmly.

"Very," outrageous Jayne said, smiling. "Very wet. I wish I could be like those porno girls. You know, with pussy juice dripping down my legs. But—well, what the fuck, why not? Okay, there we are, standing there, eighty feet tall, your cock all nice and really fucking hard, and me, pussy juice making my thighs all wet and shiny..."

She stopped as Smoke pulled off his own shirt, then bent forward to kiss, then suck, at her firmly erect nipples. Her breasts were full, plump—white, but not pale—and they jiggled slightly as Smoke worked his lips around the so-soft skin and directly on the brown nipples.

As he broke the kiss, the suck, she continued: "Yeah, eighty feet tall. People would look up and stare at us—look at us up there—very hard and wet. They'd stare and stare at us. Maybe a cab would crash, the driver not looking where he was going. Guys would get all hard, their cocks tight in their pants. Some chicks would get wet, and their nipples get really hard. But some would be all shocked and shit, trying not to look—but you know they would, 'cause their cocks and cunts would be all hard and wet, too."

Shoes, pants on the floor. Then Smoke, too. Like in her story, she was wet—though her juice didn't paint her thighs, at least not yet—and he was very, very hard. "Then we'd start to kiss, and touch each other. You'd grab my tits—oh, yeah—" her voice quavered as Smoke did just that "—and I'd wrap my hand around your cock, and slowly jerk you off."

A little bead of pre-come had dotted the head of Smoke's cock just as she'd predicted, and Jayne spread it over the tip, the head and the shaft. There wasn't a lot, but there was enough to make him slippery. Looking down at the dick in her hand, she smiled, eyes dancing over all the details of him. "—And they'd be so hard, so wet down there, watching us. Maybe a guy would start to jerk off, taking his little weenie out of his pants and beating off looking up at us on that big fucking screen. Maybe some chick would grab her tits, pulling at her nipples." Jayne did the same.

Smoke felt his heart hammering in his chest. Reaching out, he softly petted her shaven mons, enjoying—as he always enjoyed—the soft pebbled feeling of her most recent shave. Without a word, Jayne spread her legs, allowing two of his fingers to go between and up, parting her lips.

"Then I'd suck your cock. I'd get down on my eighty-feet-tall knees and take your dick in my mouth and start to suck you off...and all those people down there, they'd all be watching and they'd all start to moan. Maybe a couple of them, some freaks like us, or maybe some straights who just couldn't take it any more, would start to do it—sucking and fucking like us."

Like in her narrative, Jayne lowered herself to the dirty carpet. Kneeling, facing Smoke's long cock, she stroked it a few more times. Then she kissed the tip—tasting salt and bitter pre-come. "Maybe a couple of dyes would get down there on the street too. Skirts all pulled up, panties pushed aside, they'd eat each other's pussies—chowing down on sweet muff in the middle of Time Square. Nasty little fag boys, too: they'd get down and start sucking cock, swallowing come as they all watched me take you in my mouth, down my throat."

Then she put actions to words—carefully opening her mouth and easing Smoke's cock in and then, inch by inch, down her throat. It was a familiar game for both of them, so Smoke knew to spread his legs and push his cock down just a bit and Jayne knew to tilt her head just so.

Time stretched out, the world shrank. Smoke knew he should say something to keep the game going but his vocabulary drained out of him, whole classifications of words were lost with each inch of his cock down Jayne's throat. Still, he loved Jayne, and so he tried his best. "Yeah, oh yeah, they'd watch us. They'd watch us fuck and suck each other. The guys would be real hard, the women all fucking wet. They'd do it with us. Fuck and such each other while we did it on the big picture. Oh—"

They'd been together long enough, had done it enough, that Jayne knew when Smoke was coming close to...coming...so she pulled away, smiling up at the joy on his face. "Let me," she said, stroking him a few times. "I think I'm better at this, babe." She lost herself in Smoke's cock for a minute. "Yeah, we'd fuck for them. We'd make their day, their week, their year—they'd talk about us forever, how they'd seen us up there on that big screen. We'd be in their dreams. They'd fantasize about us—they'd jerk off to us, fuck people but think about us...for years."

As Jayne stroked him, she reached her hand around to his firm little ass and carefully hunted for his asshole. Ringing it with a fingertip, she continued. "We'd fuck our way into their heads, stud. We'd screw our way into their dreams. How would it feel to fuck five hundred people? Have all those cocks, all those cunts out there wanting you?"

Jayne licked her finger then returned to Smoke's asshole. In. In, and Smoke arched his back, exhaling harshly. Inside, Jayne positioned herself: cock in front of her eyes, finger deep in his asshole, fingers stroking plump cunt lips and then pushing inside her self, hissing as she went.

"They'd look at us, they'd want us—all of them. We'd be sex to them, we'd be New York to them. Guys would jerk off thinking of us, shooting off to what we'd done. Girls would stroke their nasty little pussies and scream out loud while dreaming of doing us." As the words came, Jayne stroked herself, and finger-fucked Smoke—staring at the gleaming, bobbing tip of his cock.

Above, Smoke moaned, low and deep, begging with wordless vowels for her lips again.

"We'd fuck for them, babe—we'd fuck for them eighty feet tall." Then she leaned forward and quickly, surely, eased his straining cock into her mouth and down her throat again.

One—he came, moaning loudly, the sound thunderous in the small room; two—a minute later as Jayne swallowed spoonful after spoonful of hot, heavy semen, she followed. One, two, their orgasms blurred their vision, clipped their muscle control. Slowly, they sank to the carpeting: Jayne sprawled on her back, breaking hard, Smoke next to her, cock still hard but none of his muscles working right. They lay there for a long time—minutes stretching into what felt like hours, the world slowly returning to them.

Finally, a word between them: "Sorry," Jayne said, shame

making her words slow and heavy. "I'm sorry." She didn't need to say more, Smoke knew it was because she couldn't bring flesh into reality. She stroked her thigh, mumbled something supportive.

More minutes—or maybe more hours, who could say? Then the door quickly opened and Truck stood there, red-rimmed eyes staring. With the door open, there was the sound of car horns and cheers from somewhere close by.

"Fuck!" Truck said, his frantic vibe falling away to deep laughter. "Fuck! The line was live—I just figured it out. Just listen to those assholes out there!"

Smoke and Jayne did, their bodies tense with shock where they lay on the floor. One—Jayne, her body shaking; two—Smoke, snorting and then howling into the ugly carpeting. Then, together, they laughed.

Truck helped them up—no stranger to seeing the two of them naked—and into their clothes. "The least you fucks can do is come up on the roof and take a bow," Truck said, beaming.

So they did: they climbed the rickety iron steps and made their way among cheap TV antennas and ventilator hoods until they stood at the edge. Below them, chaos. Below them, thousands of people. Below them, sirens and blue-and-red flashing lights.

They held hands and, stiffly at first, but then with assurance and pride, they took their bows to the thunderous cheers of Times Square.

THIN DOG

"Groove it, cooze: new *Dog's* on—" said Bodi, stretched long and manly on the Rumpus Room sofa, which responded by interpreting his posture, body lingo and pheromone secretions (even through his stylish Cordé plas unitard) and inflated itself into a warm palm bed.

"Jazz—" said Raz, dilated and staring unblinkingly at the Vid. She giggled way too high and way too long when the sofa scooped her up in its comforting presence, curled her against her manly-man, and jacked her in.

✻

Spiraling down, the audience's POV started with the ceiling-line of the room. First impression: orchestrated seedy. Too nasty to be just the fine craftsmanship of the wizards of silicone and software, the ceiling was a single slab of slightly bowed plaster, birthmarked with the strange signatures of water damage and mildew. Colors: Yellow and beige and eggshell and rust and slight, slight green. Temperature: Chill, but not too cold, a slight draft, not a door left hanging open. Smells: Predicable mildew and water, wet wood and the faint metal of cool air. The walls, to those jacked in to experience the new Vid, were the same: water-stained and mildewed. The corkscrewing descent from the ceiling was steady and slow, allowing the audience to mesh and jive with the software. The air was moving slightly, and the only sound was of a distant ceiling fan cutting the air with its blades. These sensory distractions hung in the environment a long while—masking the time it would take those with less state-of-the-art interactors to link up with the broadcast, with this slow descent into the performance stage. It was a common practice, but the techno-geeks and sly hacks behind this one were breaking new ground by using the song's build as a test pattern. It might end up an overused cliché in the years to come, but for now it was *way cool, man!*

The top of a head, and the vibrations of Thin Dog's fans could almost be felt through the network. Only one member of the quad had a head that would show up before the top of any grimy window frame. Jingo's height was well known (Interviewer on his arrival in Paris for the International Reactor Awards: "What do you think of the people of France?" Response: "Tops of heads look the same everywhere."), as was his trademarked single narrow wave of hair that went up and then down his right side in a blindingly blond cascade.

Sure enough, this member of the band's cheerfully (always) smiling face was almost completely visible before Georgina's tight black curls and Paul's tattooed (Whirlpool logo splattered on his dome in the pure blacks of tribal work—brought back into fashion by his retro statement) dome were starting to appear to the spiraling, slowly lowering audience.

Because of their various heights, the descending POV acted as a swirling introduction to the band members:

Jingo and his up-and-over blond hair; small, smiling eyes of glimmering blue; slash of a smile that, despite almost nonexistent lips, always seemed tightly sexual and humorous. Georgina and her tight forest of black, black, curls and her own round and full face (and round and full body), dancing with love and mirth and humor and the smell of turned earth—mated with her own terse and taciturn style, just as that round and firm and black, black, black body was mated with a fantastic collection of surgical steel rings (also brought back from dim rock 'n' roll antiquity, much to the love of the few remaining Primitive tribes that still roamed the badlands).

Paul and his polished dome of pure Caucasian alabaster, highlighted and emphasized by the matte black of his own ancient symbols of affiliation (GE, Apple, Shell, the eternal "Bob," Coke, and the spirit of the anti-Coke, Pepsi), lips full and red, eyes wide and same, synthetically planted old man's salt and pepper mustache—making him look off his actual twenty-seven years.

Johnna, the last, providing the dour tone with her usual dour expression: Alice Through the Looking Glass, pissed off at the world and especially that damned white rabbit; an impatient twelve-year-old girl's slender face and body inhabited by the (a lie like Paul's mustache) raging rock angst of a forty-something hard case.

You could almost feel through the electronic chorus of the net the thrill of those 2.4 billion fans as they were slowly revealed, introduced to a linked world who not only knew their names, but also their religions, favorite drugs, preferred pets, various crimes, the regularity of their body functions, the intimate details of their celebrated and notorious wild parties/orgies/birthdays/weddings/divorces, and most other minutiae of their very, very celebrated lives. The thrill of seeing them like this, slowly spiraled before their billions of fans, was like a wave crashing over a billion more reactor screens and intraneural connections. Five hundred people went into epileptic fits, three hundred thousand would seek immediate counseling, fifteen major cities would go dark from the power drain of all those tuning in, and three self-aware relay satellites in low-earth orbit would commit a fiery reentry suicide from the stress on the system.

Not bad for a band that had started out playing jazz fusion background music for hustling ragtag party girls in the Badlands.

They, and reactor tech, had come a long way since. Back

then, with the mindless dub they'd been forced to play, amid the ruins of post-Fall Bonn, they'd had an old Soviet AMG-20 truck full of equipment and had to play loud enough to cover the rumbling of the ancient diesel generator. Years and many hits later the reactor tech was all but invisible. Gone were the clumsy and backbreaking rigs, snarling cables, abrasive cranial 'trodes, body hair always getting ripped by the securing (and so Paul's bald body) tape. Now they were the top, the kings of rock 'n' roll, the gods of reactor tech. Now the 'trodes, amplifiers, dub engines, strato-implants, and translation coils were invisible and wireless—as were the couples to their nervous systems that allowed the fans, every 2.4 billion of them, to really get down and dirty in their skins as silicone hitchhikers. The fans knew—as they knew each of their drug habits, sexual positions of choice, abuse history, food issues, color of their vomit, sizes (comparatively) of their big toes—about the tracery of fine monomolecular conductors woven through their bodies, the nanotech processors inhabiting their jaws, their cortical amplifiers, and the synthesizers laced into their hipbones.

These were their instruments. And the crowd was right in there with them, along for the ride.

The spiraling POV stopped and sprang back as only a computer-controlled camera could have done, to show the folks tuned in to the sight of the room (as plain and dull as expected, all stained plaster, smooth hardwood floor, windows frosted opaque with grime, an ancient door to nowhere with a knob like a bronze mushroom, ceiling fan on its last rotations) and the four legendary Thin Dogs, in all their naked glory: Jingo, the picture of the suave rocker punk, all thin and bone, skin the color of milk with just a taste of coffee, blue eyes with wisps of mischief and rebellious energy, and hands like knotted nets—thin and strong and bony. Georgina, the black goddess, seething with the hot fire of a volcanic night; a round woman with big, round breasts; wide hips; and the shimmering lights of stainless hardware in nipples, labia, navel and *labret;* with a smile that ached to laugh a deep-throated laugh. Paul, the alabaster statue of advertising, a hairless statue of cream, no coffee, splattered and smeared with the identities of business tribes long, long gone—his were genitals familiar to them all (eleven, no fractions, inches, his fans knew by rote and worship). And Johnna the vampiric, and ultra-violent Alice, pale skin, preteen breasts, nipples like commas on a blank page, wisps between her legs, and a scowl at the world that looked ready to explode into hiss and spittle.

"Ladies and gentlemen..." a voice said offstage from the ancient past, before reactors, before the glorious tech of this glorious age, a bow to a master showman, and the originals whose work Thin Dog covered.

At once, in another display of showmanship, they turned as one to make two couples of four. Jingo to Georgina (rocker and African steel-tipped goddess), and Paul to Johnna (statuesque billboard to fairy-tale nightmare): with their first touches, the music was formed. Their movements, their contacts, leapt from skin to wires to processors to amplifiers to synthesizers and then out to the invisible studio, the overhead network of the net's satellites and receivers. They were their instruments all right, and their movements were their music:

We all need to stay together
We all need to be friends...

The gentle runnings of fingers (rocker along thick ebony skin, pale fingers cupping Alice's hip), came together and were grouped, processed and subtly changed by their hardware links and their talents for knowing exactly what to touch and when to form the notes, the chords, the tunes, the voices. And the beat, the heartbeat of good ol' fashioned rock 'n' roll, man—

They formed a fascinating tableau: rough and ready to

stainless steel highlighted goddess (he put a thin, strong hand on her full, black hip and the flow of the tune changed, adding to the song), albino billboard to possessed Alice (she leaned forward on tiptoe and kissed his full, pale lips, and a chord flowed into another, adding to the song).

Jingo bent down and kissed Georgina: a long, slow familiar kind of kiss that drew Georgina's heavy, dark arms up to Jingo's shoulders—pulling him closer, closer till large black tits, with stainless tipped nipples, touched his defined, strong (highlight of copper hair) chest. Those who cocked their heads, wiggled their fingers, or curled their toes (or any numbers of combinations they had set aside to activate the reactor tech), felt the strong lips, the cool tips of the rings, the dance of hard, wet tongues.

The POV lost it then, lost it in a spinning turn towards the famous quartet, dissolving into them. This was the miracle of the performance, this was one of the secrets of the trade. While their movements and touches sang out the notes of their tunes (in their legendary case, cover for an obscure early English band), they couldn't compete with the performance to match the tunes: they'd hurt themselves. Instead, they waltzed into their act in an intentional slow-mo—one that would come out perfectly timed and orchestrated when played back just fast enough. Jacked-in, reactor locked into this, the sensations were a blurr: feeling played at 78, not 45.

Jingo was still kissing Georgina and now they had fused into the heated gray between their two bodies, a region where strong muscles met a goddess's rolling hills and wooded forests. They were linked, locked at the mouth. The performance—this little duet—was hot and rockin'. At home in their seats all around the world, the fans could feel it too, a steam that was broadcasted from geostat satellites, smoking and churning through fiber-optical lines into homes and just about everywhere.

Yeah, but a lot of those jaded SOB's out there, who languished on their reactor couches staring off into space, into the reactor sim, just patted their yawning mouths. Seen better. Felt better. Besides, when was Thin's thing gonna start rockin'?

We all need to remember
We all need to say
Let's always be friends...

Pan, zoom, sickening drop from someplace high, down around and through and now the others were there, and with a quietness and heat that even made those jaded billions tense: Paul, pale as alabaster, as the melanin-deprived, knelt before the childish body, the proud and bold Johnna (Alice, having thrown her dress down the rabbit hole), and gently circled her bare navel (outie) with a long pink tongue.

Hands on hips, she stared down at his hairless, gleaming body with a vampire's grin—measuring him with a guillotine expression (born out by three dead lovers, nothing proven, great for the legend) as his "long pink" (all natural, as Thin Dog fans knew, despite popular myths) descended her slightly rounded belly (a bow to her acquired nature, just the right amount of baby fat that she'd had implanted) to her faint forest of slight curls. Her skin, to all and everyone plugged in, tasted of cheap soap and was so smooth as to be almost invisible. Silk? A warm breeze? Hard to tell it was even there at all.

A kiss. There, notes spilling for a second in real time, not delay. She smiled, then, and put her hands on the side of his polished, pale head. Holding? Guiding? Pushing back? The fact that she'd touched him, that fact that the ice Alice Johnna had touched a body this early in a song, made the fans sit to attention, riveted by the performance, and the rendition. She still smelled of cheap soap, but now there was the hot perfume of her cunt, slipping past the just-clean smell to tease everyone's nose. Her hair teased and tickled, a soft brush to lips and nose.

We all need to stay together,
We all need to stay together...

Pull back, twist and turn, surge of maybe nausea from the audience as their camera POV left the two and went to the other two, showing the completed tableau: Jingo was still kissing Georgina, but had moved from lips to lips. His scruffy road-trip mustache was mingling with her curly-haired bush. He was in quite deep, and she was pushing him in deeper with ringed, almost purple-black hands, so all YOU (in the reactor audience) could *see* was the forest moving, with the highlight of silver tinkling in the dark. The difference between the two was coffee and wine. Georgina was a heady perfume. A novelty and signature in a world where you could smell like roses and taste like chocolate. But hers was (as fans knew and worshipped) the modpriv, the tribal and the natural animal. God, she was a great beastie, an earth mom of soil and hot suns and eating real (gasp! gasp!) meat. Her cunt, this cunt—tickling noses and watering mouths from Alaska to Micronesia—was a cunt of babies and fucking: deep, rich and heady. The steel rings were an added spice, a pit of industrialization on good ol' Mom Earth: a coppery, steely, metallic (no duh) taste to mix with her own.

We are all the same, we are all in it together
We are all friends...

Twist and—almost—shout (too fast, man, too fast!) and we were there: Paul on his back (cool, hard boards of the floor, there but negligible because of the rest of the performance), limited vision and just the taste of cheap soap and her cunt. This time, for this number, she was champagne with a strawberry in it. A nose-tickling delicacy that perfectly matched her cherry in the folds of her origami-folded cunt. Her clit emerged under Paul's tongue, and filled the mouths of all those plugged in. Johnna's was the cunt of the age, a perfected machine for sex, as only those gene-splice wizards of the Ukraine could produce. She tasted of whatever she wanted to taste of, and her clit filled Paul's mouth like a cock: a head that swelled with the texture of strong muscles under silken skin, emerging from the delicate butterfly wings of her sculptured labia. Paul was all but blind, as were those selected for his POV; the rest saw her straddling his face, hands stroking his long, pale, also-silken, half-erection.

Each lick a note. Each gesture, each touch, each slap (ouch!) of his half-hard albino cock, was a note. This was rippin' rock 'n' roll, man—

Nothing's more important than friends...

Earth now, but not too strained and tense. This wasn't Top and Bottom, this was Man and Earth. The taste was still strong, but it was now the taste of cunt plus lips. Jingo kissed Georgina, leaning into her body, offering her the taste of cunt plus metal mixed with the taste of his mouth and hers (plus the metal of her other piercings). He was leaning into her, as she leaned up against him on her elbows. His eyes were closed (so if you wanted to get lost in that facet of the performance you could), but you could feel her tongue mixing with yours (his), batting with heated passion against the occasional click and spice of metal from her tongue and lips. And—there—her hand around his balls, worshipping, in turn, his seed and passion. Jingo grew, a feeling that those reactored-in all loved and cherished, a tightness that spread from base of cock to a jerking, tensing stiffness. Jingo getting hard was a special kind of solo, a roaring need to fuck, to Get It In. It was a rippin' performance, a roaring locomotive of stiff, iron cock.

If you chose, you could be in Georgina, and feel that steel from the outside, with the periodic insulation of rings and the aching glow of nipples excited even further by the weight of further steel. You could feel her warm cunt, the silken lips moving as Jingo moved above you. You could feel his cock in your hands, feel the tension of the muscles, the strain of it.

Each touch a note, each caress a chord. Spelling, performing—

> We're in this together,
> As only friends can be,
> We're in it together,
> You, you, you, and me...

Next to them, right next to Jingo and Georgina, were Paul and Johnna. For those in the reactor audience who hadn't switched, the action was not unexpected. But for those who'd just tuned in, or switched over, the sensation of cock being squeezed into one very tight little pussy was a shock. But not an unpleasant one, for along with her reengineered perfume, Johnna had opted for a few extras, which were working on the fucking cock of Paul: Hands? Fingers? Lips? Tongue? What was on there? It felt like someone was inside there with him, coaxing, fondling, milking his cock with each thrust into her. They were locked into a fevered doggy-style, and the reactors who'd chosen to be in the action, from Paul's point of view saw black tattoos on white skin, and Johnna's sculptured ass swallowing, fluttering like a pink tissue butterfly (more engineering) as it did, Paul's long, curved, pure white cock. He was the hot professional, and even though half, perhaps of the reactor audience was coming at his initial few thrusts, he was totally in control and was riding the wave of his near orgasm for...what...seemed...like...hours.

Inside Johnna's mind, inside her body, she was her cunt, her crafted pussy. Like an organic form of origami, the insides of her cunt were hands, ears, eyes, mouth, and body skin to her. Paul's cock wasn't just a thick tube of meat going in and out of her. She was being fucked in the hand, in the mouth, in the ass, in her clit, in her eyes (only the die-hard fans liked to watch her getting *fucked from the inside*: disconcerting to the casual viewer to see Paul ramming and withdrawing from her cunt's-eye view).

They, and Georgina and Jingo, were making beautiful music together: a harmony on several wet trombones—

We're in it together,
Friends forever,
You, you, you and me...

The performance turned into a jam, flowed and rejoined with a musical (and physical) grace that made all those critics jacked into all those reactor set-ups sit up and applaud like mad: Paul turned, swinging a crab-walking Johnna around like the beam from his searchlight. Jingo let himself get pulled by Georgina's strong cunt back and back—till the dark goddess was looking up into the pale blue eyes of wickedness, and up at the maliciously mischievous smile of Johnna. A kiss was expected as a magnet is expected to attract, so, naturally, lips met lips and tongues met tongues. Circuit made, actions magnified. They played a magnificent quartet, producing lovely music—

We all need to stay together
We all need to be friends,
We need to stand in the storm,
We need to sleep late...

The last was a unique experiment (hear those critics

applauding?): from slowed real time, a touch was a note, a special touch was a special note—as translated and picked up by all that implant technology—but now those notes were spaced by a longer time. Not a one-to-one note, but now only every third touch was a note, every fourth. The viewers, the reactors out there, felt it as a maddening flurry of speed, punctuated by the song cascading through the entire experience: a fast-forward fuck with accompanying soundtrack. Rock 'n' Roll had always, as near as anyone cared to research, been an art, a way of making music with the body, the flesh—cocks and clits and tits and ass and assholes—but this was exceptional.

Jingo and Paul knelt side-by-side, hands on cocks, hands on each other's chests, touching, kissing then, hands on each other's cocks—while before them, like a faintly undulating table, Johnna and Georgina 69'd a backbeat, a steady note for their flute playing. Reactors skipped through the performance, gliding through their sensations while the song played in the background. The hardness of Jingo's cock in Paul's hand, the salt and heat of Paul's tongue in Jingo's mouth. Johnna's cunt was aching and throbbing, as was Georgina's. Johnna's lips washed and bathed Georgina's other lips. The echo of their cunnilingus, picked up and played back through each other (they were each a cunt being eaten, a cunt to be eaten in front of them), in a crescendo of feeling, comes, music, comes, melody, and comes, comes, comes—

> We all need to be together,
> We all need to be,
> We need to be more than I,
> We so all need to be we...

The few last lines spilled with perfection as Jingo stroked the iron of Paul's cock, and Paul milked the heated come out of Jingo's long and narrow dick. Their come splashed on

Johnna and Georgina's backs, notes falling through space, ringing up the last few sounds that made the last few notes—

We all need to stay together
We all need to be friends...

✻

"Botchin'," said Bodi, frowning, stretching on the couch as it withdrew them from the Vid, disconnected them from the reactor network. "Seen better."

"Yeh," Raz said in a raspy voice, twirling Bodi's rainbow mat of chest hairs with a way-too-long finger "—but, hey, it worked, didn't it?" she added, reaching down to his bobbing cock.

"Rock 'n' Roll!" he said, smiling, and kissed her.

THE BACHELOR MACHINE

In the Pile, again—

Shoals of cubed safety glass, shimmering snow high enough to block out—or at least dazzlingly reflect—the lights of distant Austin. Like the metal underpinnings of industrial dinosaurs, cranes moved ponderously, massively in some high altitude wind above; the heads of every evolution of servicer piled in chaotic mountains, glistening blind sensors; reefs of cars, mazes of vehicles, forming avenues and alleys too tight to drive down, their mindless, picked clean corpses forcing him to walk. The phallic disappointment of an airliner fuselage crumpled at one end, smooth at the other, lay tilted and twisted and neatly pinched between a pile of burnt, blistered capsule apartments.

Friday, *again*—

—and it was raining: a hard, driving rain that seemed more to pummel him into the mud than just fall from distant, invisible clouds, as if it resented having to come such a distance only to find Kurtis at the end of its journey.

Luckily, he'd had some advance warning, wisely taking a small amount of his Thursday money to pay for three hours of net access. In those three hours he had discovered two more likely jobs, as well as learning that the government of the Sovereign Nation of Texas had changed hands yet again, the cure for Hep TCI was false, and the next day—when he traditionally wore his best—it was going to pour.

It didn't say anything at all about *hammer*.

Still, he'd had some notice—enough to wrap himself from

his fake California clone-leather shoes to his one-size-too-small fake European suit in a Walking Bag™. The rain was like a perpetually full bucket spilling onto his head, blinding him to everything except the hardest lights of the Pile, turning its yellow dirt into sole-sucking mud, and shoving him down just about to his knees—but at least he wasn't wet.

LOVE in red biolight so dark it came close to purple. Pulsing even through the static-sounding rain, glowing past its distorting pour. There may have been, at one time, something before LOVE or after LOVE but that side of the place was gone—cropped off by a cliff of compressed cars and an imprecise pyramid of refrigerators. LOVE was lopsided, tilted, twisted—barely able to glow. Whoever had made it had, despite the natural laws of the universe, made LOVE last.

Once, the front had been a plastic display of eroticism. Organiform...no, *sensual* form, the exterior showed curves and dips, dimples and swells that might once have architecturally echoed the subtle contours of a woman. The door was a protruding dome, the knob a brass spiral that could have been a nipple. The front was a play of gentle slopes and heavy overhangs with a frozen fleshy weight to them. Along the bottom was a fringe of brilliant pink plastic, like lips dragging on the ground—hiding, no doubt, the unit's tires, the service's ability to pick itself up and move on when a neighborhood or a town tired of it.

When LOVE had run its course for them.

Once it had been a paradise of sexual form and enticing design. But it was in the Pile, now. The fleshy contours were now sad and mildewed. Like acne, vacant gaps told where smaller, pocketable details had been wrenched free. Like cellulite, supposedly eternal plastics had sagged under industrial-strength weather and persistent gravity. The door was yellowed and streaked, clouded till it revealed nothing at all of LOVE's interior—a tawdry shawl for a very old and unwanted edifice.

As Kurtis stepped up, the door pneumatically opened with a gasp and an irritating grating of mud and sand caught in some mechanism—that put LOVE as far away as dry on that rainy day. The foyer had once been plush and decorative, an attempt to recall the elegance and promise of a historical bordello. Red velvet, antique prints of ladies in daring positions and strong postures. Tassels and gold ropes. A vase of brilliant roses. Now, though, it was all covered with a thick coat of yellow dust, the floor bore hardened mud inches deep. The roses were plastic and out-of-focus from dust and spider webs. The once red velvet wall-wrappings and the once thick shag looked like they'd been in the stateroom of a lady of dubious repute on the *Titantic*—*after* it had sunk and been on the bottom for years.

The main room was mostly lost to soft but deep shadows. Calmly unzipping his bag, Kurtis climbed out and carefully folded it so that the dry inner lining wouldn't touch anything in the place and put it down on a red velvet chair with only three legs, propped against a built-in couch and covering a low hill of disposable sunjoy syringes.

One door. Padded leather gutted by a impressionist series of slashes, yellowed stuffing puffing out like geometric fungus. Over the door was a red indicator. As Kurtis glanced up it flickered, pulsed, then lit: AVAILABLE.

The room beyond was dark and smelled of hot plastic, ozone, and mildew. There was one window, a porthole that leaked in a grainy light from the Pile's hard industrial lights filtering through the storm—it splashed a crisp oval on the bed, showing a plastic ankle and the top of a red-spangled pump.

"Hello there, Sugar," said tones that had once been melting butter, scintillating sugar, a purring kitten from the top of the bed, lost to shadows—but had since evolved through countless breakdowns, missed upgrades, and general disuse into a scratching, wheezing of sounds that could, or could not have been actual words.

"Um, er, ah—hello?" Kurtis said, looking up and around for the lights, thinking that he might have to do some banging around to get them to work.

"Hello there, Sugar."

The ceiling was high. Too high to reach, even if he wanted to risk climbing the stances of the high four-poster bed that took up most of the room.

"H-h-hello, Ssssssugar..."

A heavy click, and a thud that Kurtis felt through his fake shoes—a sound exactly like someone giving one of the plastic walls a hefty smack, then: "Looking for love, honey?"

A chime, like glass heated too fast. The first flash of light showed the room clearly, like a pop of lightning: bed with satin canopy, chair—toppled and broken, table—listing, bric-a-brac (small lamp in the shape of a stretching deco nymph, glass jar of some unnamable liquid) frozen, glued, to its tilted surface), and a painting of an overly developed woman reclining on a flowered sofa.

"Um, er, yeah—" Kurtis said, feigning innocence but, because the smell of the place—mildew and ozone from frying electronics—was making him faintly nauseous, not doing a very good job of it.

Another chime. Another blast of pure, white light from the biolights overhead. She moved from her "sultry" and "provocative" position on the bed, forward till she was sitting on the edge, looking over her next client: "Are you a virgin, by any—*hummm*—chance?"

"Um, I guess you could say so. I mean I haven't done it with a...um, before..." Kurtis said, feeling stupid and hot with embarrassment. He said the words with the conviction of a underpaid actor, then smiled at the tilted truth of that and laughed a bit to himself.

"You are in good hands, sweetie. Very good hands," she

said, moving with misfiring, hesitant steps off the bed and out of the shadows as the lights surged one last time before dropping down to their designed "intimate bedroom" glow that made the room look like it was at the bottom of a crimson-watered lake.

Her face was plastic, a pink and rouged mask, and moved with glacial expressions in response to motors under the stiffening and cracking skin. Her eyes were glass or some kind of clear material, and when they moved they jerked from one seen object to another: Kurtis's face, his body, his crotch.

Her hair had slipped to one side, once golden curls now faded white way beyond the elderly Greta Garbo—she was half bald. Her mouth didn't move when she talked; instead it hung, half open, showing a bright red sheet of plastic, spongy tongue.

She was tall, a fact that always surprised Kurtis—no matter how many times he saw her. For some reason he always initially expected her to be smaller, less threatening in her misfiring and stuttering movements. Maybe it was his memory that was misfiring more—and it was only in his faulty retrospect that she was diminutive, with larger, deeper eyes.

Her body was leggy and exaggerated—as if her designers had seen their true opportunity and instead of trying to imitate a real person they realized a broad icon. If she were flesh and blood instead of polymnemonic alloys, resin composite, fiber threads, and biosmart circuits she would be a hopeless victim of gravity. Instead she was firm and shaped in ways that no flesh woman could be. She was a Vargas, a playing card, a calendar, a T-shirt.

Her breasts were almost bare, hardly hidden by her shift. They were—he admitted to himself, carefully keeping his eyes from her face and its malfunctioning rigor—more than just quite nice. Plastic, yes, used and abused by god knew how many clients since it had been given its own unique semblance of life by a division of Lovelife, Inc. some twenty-five years previously.

Kurtis took off his coat, hoping that the rest of her wasn't misfiring as badly as her voice, and draped it carefully on the bag.

"Oh, you're a handsome one—" she purred, her voice not quite coming from her mouth, as she stepped up close to him.

Close, his eyes locked on her imperfections, her broken parts. The smell of mildew and fried circuits was powerful, scraping the inside of his sinuses. The world became, then, a walk uphill. It wasn't just another Friday. Instead, he faced too many hours till the end of it. It was almost like a physical pain, an ache in his belly and back at the thought of going through the minutes, maybe even the hour to get to the end of it.

It wasn't just her, despite her misfiring and deteriorated condition, because what was rolling heavy and mean through his mind wasn't just the work for that afternoon—it was everything. His life. His age. His income. His shoes.

His shoes. In the space of the moment the feelings took to roll through him he looked over at his coat and then down at the shoes still on his feet. Fake. Not cheap, but still fake. He was proud of his shoes, proud that he looked nice on Fridays.

He looked at her, saw her for what she was—broken. Once she was new, state-of-the-art. People came from all over to indulge themselves with her.

But now it was raining outside. Her carpets were caked with the yellow mud of the Pile and the future wouldn't bring anything but deeper mud on her once-fine carpets.

And Fridays. The one thing that perhaps made her circuits warm was Fridays. Fridays and Kurtis.

Somewhere in these thoughts, Kurtis felt some of the weight lift. Much of it was still there, but then it was replaced with a wry sense of warmth, a glow of self-satisfaction. How bad could it fucking be? he thought. At least I don't have someone just like me to look forward to.

Her eyes, shining buttons, looked straight at him and right then, he felt like she was looking up at him, and not down.

"Very fine," she said, her volume failing. "Has anyone told you that you're very handsome?"

"No, not really," he said, with a firmness that was totally opposed to his usual role.

"Well more people should," she said, "because I sure think it's true." She was wearing a simple shift, a once-white synthetic silk gown that draped tight over her large, perfectly conical breasts and fell just above her feet. As she walked, they swung, heavy and firmer than any real woman's ever could be and her nipples, on an electronic cue, hardened under the soft but stained, torn, *used* material.

Her movements were haltingly fluid, an action he never could have envisioned till he saw her. It was as if her normal ballet of getting up off the bed and walking over to him was given an internal quake of misfiring motors: a dancer with a muscular stammer. "You know," she said, in a smiling tone that was totally beyond her normal banter, "I know this is business and all, but at least it is a business I enjoy."

Oh, for god's sake, Kurtis thought, *just get on with it.* What he said, though, was a slighting acidic, "Me, too, hon. I mean it."

"Flatterer," she said, trying to smile. Her frozen lower jaw buzzed then clicked together savagely, making Kurtis's cock freeze in his pants. "Should charge extra for that—" Now her jaw was working better, synching its action with her voice.

She was next to him, standing too close. Her hand, middle finger slightly hesitant as, he guessed, its motors were going, flattened and gently rested against his chest. "I specialize in first timers, you know—" she said, following the script again. "There's nothing to be afraid of. We're going to have fun, hon—*lots* of fun."

"Thank you, ma'am," Kurtis said, looking down at her.

"Like I said, honey—the pleasure's going to be mine as

well." Her hand dropped, brushing the front of his pants, pausing over the lack of a bulge. "Nervous?"

"Well, yeah, kind of—" Kurtis said, gently trying to move her hand away from his crotch, get her away from his failure.

"There's nothing to be ashamed of, sweetheart," she said, taking his hand and pulling him toward the bed.

It was dusty, dirty, with a thicker coat since the last time he'd been on it. His shoes. "Wait a minute," he said, and went back over to the Walking Bag™. Shoes. Pants. They all went on the plastic. In his socks, underwear, and shirt, he went back to the bed. Investment protected.

Her head was down slightly, as if she'd diverted her gaze from his step beyond the fourth wall of their routine. Sitting back down on the bed, she seemed to look at him: the shy virgin and not Kurtis from countless Fridays. "It's all right to be shy, even scared. It's the same for many people—there's nothing to be ashamed of. Believe me, I understand." The words were smooth and kind, even though her voice was hard and crackling. "I'm here to help you, to make you feel good. That's what this is all about—having fun and feeling good. I want you to be comfortable, to relax. I won't do anything that's going to hurt you. If I do, you just say so and I'll stop right away."

"Thank you," he said, looking at her eyes for some reason. Glistening plastic.

"Do you like the way I look? Do you like to look at me?" she arched her back, showing her artificial breasts to their ancient-designer perfection. Nipples like fingertips, harder, redder than any human woman's. One foot was cocked up near her lap and he noticed that the skin there was cracked, split—showing a braid of amber fibers and the dull shine of a polycarbon alloy shin.

"Yes." Her skin was not quite human, the luster having been removed after thousands of men's hands had touched her, fucked her. Even cutting edge technology becomes dull and lackluster after having been...used for too long. That middle finger hesitated and clicked again as she moved her hand up his leg, inching towards his cock. The lie was sharp and impatient on his lips.

"Would you like to see my breasts?" Her head was gently tilted down and looking up at him with a coy expression.

"Yes, I would," he said, surprised by the softness in his words. There had been innocence in her voice—buzzing and clicking—that had pushed away the industrial reality of her form.

With a too-feminine gesture, she slipped the straps of her gown off and brought her hands together, holding the weight of her breasts. Reaching down, she took one of his hands and put it on the warm slope of her left breast. Many hands, many fucks, but the texture was just about right, a hair's breadth from being a real woman's.

"I like my breasts. I think they're pretty. Do you like them, too?"

"Yes—yes, I do," he said. The rain had stopped and the sun had come out. A hard beam of sunlight struck her face and, for a moment, he watched the dust motes from the stuffy room drift past her clear eyes.

She took one hand away, leaving his on the swell of her breast. Under his thumb, unconsciously or accidentally resting there, he felt her nipple harden even more, grow even hotter.

Her hand was on his crotch, slowly stroking his cock. Distantly, he realized he was getting hard.

"It's okay—it really is. It's all right to get excited, to feel the way you do—"

*Come on, just get it over with...*he thought, with a flush of anger.

"—you just have to relax and do what feels good." She was stroking his cock—very hard—deftly, with the accuracy of a lathe, a piece of factory-floor machinery, but with the programmed skill of a world-class courtesan. "Now then, doesn't this feel good?"

"It does," he said sharply, irritated with himself that his hand was stroking her breast, teasing and circling the nipple with his finger. He was tempted to pinch it, to squeeze too hard... but didn't. Partially because he needed the work, but also because he suspected she wouldn't, or couldn't, complain.

His cock was out and rock hard. It felt like it was happening to someone else, someone with a body just like his own but a million miles away. That same person had lifted her breast and was enjoying the weight of it. That same person had his lips an inch or two away from a plastic, artificial nipple.

"You want to suck? Please—go right—*hummmmmm*—ahead. I like that."

He kissed it. Expecting dust, oil, stale plastic, Kurtis was surprised by faint salt. Trying to think about the subtle technology required for the parlor trick, he lost his train of though as she stroked his cock with deft gestures.

"I remember this one boy. He must have slipped out of his house to come—he was kind of scared of the time, you know? He was so nervous but so sweet. I remember he had this faint little mustache, like rust on his upper lip. Pale face, with lots of freckles. He could have been older, I suppose, but I think he was young. That I was his first.

"He was so scared. At first I thought it was because of me, you know—some people have had a real hard time putting what I am aside. Others, of course, got off on it. I thought that he was scared of getting caught in the gears. But he was just shy—scared of women. I tried the usual things to get him relaxed but he was just too frightened. But he didn't leave, see?

"So I talked to him. I put him in that chair—" broken and leaning, dimmed by the dust "—and I just talked to him. I told him that it was okay to feel the way he was, that loving women, or men for that matter, is nothing to be frightened or ashamed of. I offered myself, holding his hand and speaking softly, but I also told him that if he didn't want to then we wouldn't. We just talked. When my time was up and he had to go he gave me a hug and cried a little bit."

His cock was hard. He was surprised by how hard. *Damn,* he thought, *fucking good programming!* As she'd spoken, going beyond her usual lines, he'd licked and kissed at her nipple, feeling its almost-perfect texture on his lips and with his tongue.

With a gentle hand on his chest, she pushed and guided him down onto the bed. Distantly, something told him he should be taking his shirt off—so he stopped her with a cold expression on his face, got up, and neatly folded it on top of his other clothes. Standing tall and rigid he walked back to the bed.

Again she pushed him down. He let himself be pushed, but with a bit of strength in his spine, a little protest.

Her mouth may have been malfunctioning but the skill with which she used it...pressure, wetness, texture, the play of all of that, and the soft weight of her large breasts on his lap... Misfiring aside, still she was once cutting edge, state-of-the-art. Her program was fine, her skill...adept.

Up on his knees, watching with grim interest as her plastic head slid up and down on the shaft of his cock, he felt his eyes waver, his heart pound. Sliding down, he lay back and closed his eyes—lost to the swirling action or her artificial tongue, her plastic teeth, her foam and perplex throat, the complex series of molecules designed to give him the best sensation with superb lubrication. His groin ached, his cock was beyond throbbing and had—quickly, damned quickly—rocketed up to that wonderful agony, that good hurt of balls pressurized from her action on his shaft and head. His breathing was rocky and quick and Kurtis found himself mumbling things, whispering and grunting half-words and fragments of sounds as her actions grew more and more rough, more and more intense.

Fucking soon...

Before he was even aware of it she was slowing easing back, her actions becoming gentler, softer. The pressure in his balls was there, dangerously so, but it wasn't a cliff he was running off but rather a hill he could roll down. Then it was a cool wash on his cock and balls and his heart was thudding regularly. Then the ache dropped down to a slow throb.

"I remember this one time," she said, plastic smile at his bobbing cock. "A guy brought his girlfriend to me. Said that she wanted to try it with girls. Oh, my—you wouldn't believe the times I've told guys about women, and being with them. But I hadn't you see—just stories to get them off. I had the knowledge, you know, but not really the—" her chuckle sounded like something had broken down deep inside of her, something grating "—experience. At first I was, you know, not sure about this. Like, maybe, the girl wasn't into this at all, that she just had this pushy boyfriend.

"But her eyes. She liked looking at me. Liked touching me. I kept it simple, that time, just some kissing and letting her feel my breasts, my pussy. I could tell she wanted more but I kept seeing him, looking at us. There was something in his eyes I didn't like, something that kept moving between seeing us having fun and us not needing him."

Getting up, she slipped off the rest of her dress. The skin around her stomach was wrinkled like something in her internal workings had slipped down and was almost pressing out of her plastic skin. Her thighs, too, looked like the skin was about to break and as she moved, climbing with sudden bursts of misfiring hesitancy onto him, he could see flashes of optical circuits through the stretched plastic.

Kurtis closed his eyes, tried to think about money through his aching cock, and leaned back.

"Later—" he felt his cock touch her lips. Cool. Not cold at

least. Some thermal function not quite working. Wet, though. Very. He felt her lips part gently as she held herself over his cock. Straining, he felt himself move gently against them, sliding on the slippery fluid of her cunt. "—I saw her again. She came to me when he was out of town. She was more than interested but was so scared. I was parked at his mining town, you see—one of those Latter Day Saints enclaves, you know? They didn't like me being there but at least they were able to look the other way—clink, clank, clunk, right? Sex with a piece of equipment is better than sex with a person." Sadness? So many years of giving pleasure only to end up in the Pile? "She came back. I saw her a lot. Once a week for a while. She was so enthusiastic, like she was starving. Then her unit was sold off to the Amazon Reclamation Project and I never saw her again."

Her weight was on him and his cock— pulsing shaft and shimmering head—eased up inside of her wet warmth; at least inside her heat was working. She swallowed him up inside her, pushing herself down on top of him to get as much of his cock into her as she could. As she did her own words broke and fragmented—turning into soft grunts and vowels. With her head tilted back, her too-perfect-for-flesh breasts hanging big and soft in front of him, she brought her feet up next to him and pulled herself up softly, as if enjoying the action of his cock sliding out as much as she had feeling it slid in.

"She gave me a rose. She paid for a full hour just to run in and give me a rose. It was a fake one and she was so ashamed of that. Couldn't find a real one, she said. I thought it was perfect, though—and told her so. Just perfect."

She started up move up and down on his cock, pumping herself up and down and him in and out. Kurtis's body quaked with her meticulous up and down action. His balls again throbbed with the need for release—a fine, ecstatic ache.

Damn, he found himself thinking, *she's fucking good....*

"An old man came to me once. He'd taken PassOn™ — had

something incurable he said, didn't want to feel the pain. I didn't know what to do—" Sadness? Thinking of him? Knowing that she wouldn't have any more like him? Now, old and obsolete, so it was just Kurtis every Friday? Just Kurtis so she could feel like she was needed, wanted again. The programmers had been too good, too skilled. She liked what she did, but now was too old—except for Kurtis every Friday. "—so we kissed and I held him.

"Then he talked. He told me all of the horrible things he'd thought or done. I don't really know if they were all that bad, I don't know those kinds of things, but he certainly did. He cried as I held him. Finally he said he wanted to go feeling good and empty—and he couldn't tell anyone else he loved the things he told me. He wanted to tell the truth for once, to let it all out to someone who would still love him after."

Her actions were clear and crisp but there was something else, a kind of shiver as she brought herself up and down. As she talked, her voice laced with less and less *buzzes, clicks, whirrs* and *humms,* she moaned and groaned more and more from her actions, from the feeling of him inside her. Her hands went to her breasts and stroked and felt their shape before landing on her nipples. Taking them between thumb and forefingers she pulled them, hard—much harder than he ever would have—turning their round beauty into stressed cones. Her voice, still speaking, became rough and ragged—chopped with hard vowels from their fuck.

"We made love, the old man and I. When we were done he didn't have that much time. He kissed me and left. Later I found out that he'd died out on the street, two steps from my door. The funeral was big. Many people came and I guess they cried. I know I would have, cried tears and watched him go into the ground, too—if I could."

Kurtis felt her thighs slap down into his own, felt her cunt—expertly constructed—envelop and constrict around his cock. He felt her internals massage and work him, milking the come out of his body. Leaning forward, she let go of her nipples and dropped down to drape her breasts, heavy and hot, in his face. Something rough and feeling almost broken rested in his chest but he didn't care. He heard something deep inside her grate and squeak with a sudden lack of lubrication. He might have cared, might even have been frightened—but he was too far gone, too far beyond the edge. The hill was far beyond him and the edge of the cliff was coming up fast—

He exploded, fireworks of a wet and organic variety as he jetted into her synthetic cunt. His body jerked and shook with the power of his orgasm, a rocket that shot up from his balls to his shaft and out the head. Stars, lightheadedness, the closeness to god and death—the usual clichés of a powerful, mind-altering come.

Feeling somewhere else, somewhere distant and fuzzy, she neatly cleaned him up with a washcloth and helped him to his feet. Quiet, silent, she rubbed his back and he tried to form thoughts that would lead to the action of putting on his pants, shoes, shirt and coat. Finally enough of his brain was behaving itself to allow him to actually turn intent into action—and he did.

"What do I owe you?" Eyebrows designed to show lust, artificial lips created for sensation and beauty looked sad and old. Eyes designed for seeing and for showing interest looked cold and remote. Her voice was hollow, stilled: "Two hundred?"

"Three," Kurtis said, more from reflex. Rather than look in her eyes, at the plastic, he carefully noticed a bit of wayward fluff on his pants, brushed it off.

"I—I don't think—" the device sighed, a heavy, vast sound as if it came from some great bellows hidden in the depths of her body. "Three then."

Kurtis collected his three hundred, swiping his card through an ornate terminal she produced, then left—trying not to look back, not to think too much as he did.

⁂

It was raining again. With an embarrassed shock he realized, standing in it, feeling it dot his face with chilled drops, that he hadn't put on his bag, that it was still neatly folded over his arm.

Stepping into the protection of an overhang caused by the twisted metal corpse of an Aeroflot delivery van that had somehow been shoved slightly out of the vast wall of crushed vehicles, he struggled and fought with the bag till it was on.

Then he took out his debit card and cleared the credits she'd paid him for his attention, to feel like she was wanted again—returned it all. Every cent. *Thanks for those that didn't get to say so.* The words might not have been there, in his mind, but the feelings were. Then he pulled up the hood on his bag, zipped it and walked away—till the next week.